Where would they be safe?

Out of the corner of her eye, Amy saw a closed door to what looked like a small storage closet. But as she turned toward it, she ran directly into an unmoving chest.

Large hands clamped on both of her shoulders, surrounding Elaina and stopping her midstep. "Amy? Are you all right? I thought I heard someone screaming."

She had to peer all the way up into his face to get a good look at Jordan, but even then her eyes wouldn't quite focus on him.

"Amy." His tone was clipped, his eyes darting from her to Elaina and back. "What's wrong?"

Everything in her melted. She hadn't even known she'd wanted his help, but now that he was here, she recognized him for exactly what they needed. "Someone's chasing us. Shot at us."

If he needed to think through his actions, it took him only a fragment of a second. He grabbed them both, shifting them out of the line of view of the stairwell. "Stay right here. Don't move."

By day **Liz Johnson** works as a marketing director. She makes time to write late at night and is a two-time ACFW Carol Award finalist. She lives in Tucson, Arizona, and enjoys exploring local theater and doting on her nieces and nephews. She writes stories filled with heart, humor and happily-ever-afters and can be found online at www.lizjohnsonbooks.com.

Books by Liz Johnson

Love Inspired Suspense

Men of Valor

A Promise to Protect
SEAL Under Siege
Navy SEAL Noel
Navy SEAL Security
Hazardous Holiday
Christmas Captive

Witness Protection

Stolen Memories

The Kidnapping of Kenzie Thorn
Vanishing Act
Code of Justice

Visit the Author Profile page at Harlequin.com.

CHRISTMAS CAPTIVE

LIZ JOHNSON

HARLEQUIN® LOVE INSPIRED® SUSPENSE

Recycling programs for this product may not exist in your area.

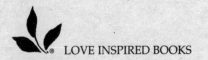 LOVE INSPIRED BOOKS

ISBN-13: 978-0-373-67854-9

Christmas Captive

www.Harlequin.com

Printed in U.S.A.

We love Him, because He first loved us.
−1 John 4:19

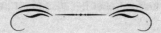

For Amy, the best kind of friend.
I'm so thankful for you!

And for all of the second chance sweethearts,
whose love is richer because of forgiveness.

ONE

When Petty Officer Jordan Somerton stepped onto the lido deck of the cruise ship *Summer Seas*, he'd have gladly given a month's salary to be on land.

That wasn't something he usually thought. Not after almost ten years in the navy, eight of those as a SEAL. Sea. Air. Land. It didn't matter to him on any given mission. He was comfortable in any and all.

Only this wasn't a mission. And he wasn't aboard a naval ship.

"Jordan!" his aunt Phyllis called from the starboard side of the hardwood deck. As she waved her hand, enough bracelets to sink a liner half this size jangled around her wrist. He wasn't usually called Jordan by anyone but his family. His team called him River. As in the Jordan River.

But he didn't think he could avoid Aunt Phyllis by pretending he didn't recognize his own name. Not with her eyes on him like a laser. So he smiled at her and circled around the outskirts of the crowd, his back always to the wall, facing the collection of Somertons and Sutcliffs mingling around the pool.

A ship with a pool. What a waste of space.

But Aunt Phyllis didn't seem to agree. She shuffled over, dragging his youngest cousin, Stephanie, in her wake.

"Hi, Steph," he said, leaning down to hug her shoulders and kiss the top of her head. Even though she had just graduated from high school, their standard greeting seemed fitting since he'd spent most of his growing-up years living with them. "How's college?"

She shrugged, but it did nothing to dim the smile on her lips and her flashing white teeth. "Okay."

Phyllis pouted. "She met a young man and wants to go to his house for Christmas."

Stephanie's eyes bugged out. "Mo-om!"

Jordan tried not to laugh, but Stephanie's face was just too good to hold it back. "Sorry, kiddo. Welcome to being an adult single in this family. I wish I could tell you it gets better." He shook his head. "It doesn't."

She glanced toward the corner of the pool, where Stephanie's sister and her fiancé stood, hand in hand, staring into each other's eyes. A little too in love for his taste.

"But they never teased Kaneesha."

"It's because she's been dating Rodney since they were thirteen. Everyone's known this week was coming forever." He just hadn't been planning on their wedding taking place on a cruise ship somewhere in the middle of the Caribbean a week before Christmas. "Just wait until you bring a guy home." He rolled his eyes. "I can't wait to see that!"

Phyllis was already frowning, clearly picturing her baby walking down the aisle. Suddenly her eyes shifted in Kaneesha's direction. "Speaking of bringing a date to family dinner…"

Her voice trailed off and his stomach hit the deck. Rodney, in his sharp gray suit, took a step to the side as a third person joined them.

Amy Delgado. Long brown hair flowing behind her. Full skirt dancing around her knees in the ship's breeze. Bright pink lips curved in an overflowing smile.

Words failed him.

She was stunning. And he would have noticed that, with or without the elbow to his ribs from Phyllis. He grunted. She pouted.

"I can't believe you let that one get away."

Yeah, yeah, yeah. He knew. He'd botched

that. Badly. And he didn't blame Amy for hating him.

The broken date hadn't been entirely his fault. He'd blame that on the Lybanian terrorist who had suddenly popped out of hiding and tried to take over an otherwise peaceful village where a slew of American aid workers had set up shop. When the US government called on him to do his job, he'd done it. Even if it meant breaking a date he'd kind of been looking forward to.

But the lead-up to it—the *before*-the-date misunderstanding in front of his entire family that had required an apology date—that was all on him.

He was lost somewhere in the memory when Neesha waved at him. "Come over here."

No. That was a bad idea. Because Amy was staring at him now, too. And putting the two of them together never ended well. But when the bride called, he'd go running.

"Neesha, you look beautiful." He greeted her with a kiss on the cheek before shaking his soon-to-be cousin-in-law's hand. Then he shoved his own into the pocket of his black slacks.

But his cousin wasn't about to be so easily mollified. She stared at him like a sniper's spotter, her gaze intense and lips in a stern line. He made a silly face, hoping to distract her from that frown before Aunt Phyllis saw it.

The bride should always be smiling, she'd scolded him before they left the port in Miami. *So I don't want to hear a word about how much you hate cruise ships. Understood?*

Yes, ma'am, he'd said, because any good South Carolina boy knew better than to argue with the woman who had raised him without complaint since he was six.

But his faces didn't do a thing to change Kaneesha's grumpy expression or alter her reproachful tone. "Amy said you haven't practiced your dance yet. You know all of the bridesmaids and groomsmen are joining us for the second dance, and I don't want it to be your first time dancing together."

He met Amy's dark brown gaze over Neesha's shoulder. Though her eyes said she wasn't particularly pleased to see him, she still mouthed an apology for landing him in hot water. It was quite possibly the first time she'd ever apologized to him. He was the one with all the practice in that department. But he wasn't fooled into believing that this meant they were on the same team. In fact, he was pretty sure they were playing different sports. And whatever this was, he was perpetually three steps behind.

Between Amy's cold shoulder and his family's nagging, he knew there was no chance he was getting away from this trip without making everyone mad at him, one way or another. That's why he'd prefer being in the field. At least then he had a clear objective—and a team to back him up if he ever got in over his head.

"Are you even listening to me?"

He jerked his mind back to his cousin. "Of course I am."

Kaneesha narrowed her eyes and put her hands on her hips. "Uh-huh." Jordan's attention shifted back to Amy. The gold highlights in the navy blue dress made her deep brown skin glow, and the highlights in her wavy hair shone in the late-afternoon sun.

"It's good to see you, Amy."

She nodded, the briefest acknowledgment. Then asked, "How's Will?"

Of course she'd ask about his SEAL teammate. She'd been friends with Will Gumble for years. The fact that she'd barely acknowledged Jordan's status as anything more than a barnacle on the hull of a ship meant they hadn't progressed past prolonged apologies.

"He's fine. Jess is about to pop. Will's pretty excited about being a dad."

She offered a flicker of a smile. He knew she still took credit for getting Will and Jess back together after ten years apart. And he had to give Amy credit. As a DEA agent, she'd been able to get Will set up with a false identity and thrown into a drug cartel's compound where Jess had been held captive. Working together under the noses of their captors, they'd managed to save the day—and Will had won Jess over.

Suddenly their foursome became five, as a young girl bounded up to them from the dance floor.

"There you are!"

All four adults turned to the girl, whose pink cheeks couldn't hide her delight or the effects of the brisk wind. And Amy's eyes, always so expressive, grew round. "Elaina, what are you doing here?" She gracefully dipped to look the girl Jordan recognized as her eight-year-old niece in the eye. "I thought your dad took you back to your suite after dinner."

Elaina shrugged. "I came to find you. I didn't want to stay in my room." A shadow of doubt crossed her face, and she reached for Amy's hand. "My dad had to make a secure call from the captain's office again. I was lonely."

Neesha's smile blossomed, and she bent to give Elaina a hug. "We can't have our flower girl spending the evening all alone. Come on." With a tug, she led Elaina and Rodney toward the dance floor and began to spin.

Amy crossed her arms as her gaze narrowed on her niece, and Jordan could do nothing but shove his hands deeper into his pockets, unsure what to say.

After a long pause, she spoke, barely loud enough to be heard over the thumping music coming from the DJ in the corner. "I worry about her. Ever since her mom died, it just seems like Michael is working more and more."

Jordan nodded. Not that she deigned to glance in his direction.

"It's hard for a little girl when her dad isn't around."

He knew she had some personal experience on that front. Her parents had split when she was young, and her dad hadn't really been a part of her life. But despite a nearly twenty-year history between them—she was Neesha's best friend after all—she'd never talked about it with him. Their conversations had rarely dipped below the surface.

Fair was fair, though—it wasn't as if he'd ever chosen to confide in her. She knew about the circumstances of his childhood—messed up as it had been—because Neesha couldn't keep from spilling every single bean she had. But it didn't mean they talked about it. Ever.

Amy's soft voice pulled him from his thoughts again.

"I tried really hard…but when Michael was sent to Lybania and I was transferred…"

Yeah, he knew that Michael Torres was now the US ambassador to Lybania. Jordan had actually met him after the mission that forced Jordan to cancel his sort-of date with Amy. But he couldn't admit that he'd met Amy's brother-in-law before this cruise. Not when the mission was still classified.

"Mmm-hmm." It was more grunt than acknowledgment, but it was enough for her to jerk her head up, her gaze sharp and surprised, like she'd forgotten who she was talking to.

"You don't have to pretend like you want to listen to me." Her tone wasn't bitter, but there was a distinct crispness in her words.

"I'm not pretending." If they could smooth over so many months of awkwardness between them just by talking about other people, he'd be happy to listen to her for hours. But he knew it wasn't that simple. Even if neither of them wanted to talk about it, they still needed to address the elephant on the lido deck. Rubbing the top of his head, he stared at his shoes for a long moment. "Listen, Amy, I'm—"

With a swift wave of her hand, she cut him off. "Please don't. We've been through this enough times. You've apologized. Your teammates have apologized on your behalf. I'm just surprised that you haven't sent your pastor to apologize."

He tried for a laugh, but it came out dry and throaty and wholly unlike his normal chuckle.

When she looked into his eyes, hers were sure and unflinching. "I accept your apology." Only her tone suggested the exact opposite.

"But we can't be friends?"

"I think it's better if we aren't. Don't you?"

She didn't give him time to answer. She just stalked in Neesha's direction, flashing a smile at Elaina as she danced across the hardwood floor, leaving him to wonder if he'd ever get a second chance.

He wasn't used to accepting defeat. Especially not after battling through the rigors of the BUD/S—Basic Underwater Demolition/ SEAL—training. He'd been pushed to his limits both mentally and physically, and ever since then, giving up hadn't been part of his MO. Throwing in the towel on whatever he and Amy could have been didn't sit well with him.

They were stuck in a floating party together for five more days, so he might as well spend the time figuring out how to get her to really forgive him.

"Rodney can dance!"

"Not as well as you." Amy laughed, spinning Elaina around the dance floor as a DJ played her favorite Cyndi Lauper song from the 80s.

Elaina threw her head back and smiled up at the sky as it faded to ink, her stick-straight hair swinging wide around her shoulders. "Can we do this all night?"

"No." Amy gave Elaina her best fake-stern look. She had a real stern one, too. But she saved that for drug runners and cokeheads with big guns.

"Oh, please. I don't want to go back to my room." There was a slight tremor in the girl's voice that put Amy on her guard. Elaina wasn't the type to whine. If she said something was wrong, she meant it.

"Why not?" Amy knew for a fact that Elaina and her father—and their bodyguard—were staying in one of the very best suites on the ship.

The girl looked up, then down at her feet. "My dad's not there and it…it feels like someone's watching me."

The hairs on the back of Amy's neck jumped to a salute. Helping Elaina make a more controlled turn so she didn't bump into the other dancers peppered across the floor, Amy picked out her next question carefully. "Has your dad been leaving you alone? Has he had to make a lot of calls?"

Elaina shrugged but turned it into a shimmy as the music hit a faster beat. "This is the fourth time since we left. Probably something for work."

Amy mimicked her niece's movements, but with her mind engaged elsewhere, she was always a half a beat behind the music.

She couldn't picture anything but her brother-in-law's face. His dark hair had turned gray at the temples, and she couldn't be sure if it was from Alexandra's battle with cancer or his new role for the State Department. His smile, which had captivated Alex from the start, had turned haggard.

Amy stared at her niece, her features so much like Alex's had been. But Elaina's eyes were shadowed, haunted.

Amy knew Michael's focus on work had Elaina feeling lonely and neglected, but this didn't seem like mere sadness. Elaina actually seemed afraid. Could she be right about someone watching her? But who? And why?

The girl yawned loudly.

Maybe she was just tired.

But there was something about the way her voice shook when she said she felt like she was being watched. As far as cruise ships went, this was a fairly small specimen. But there were still enough people aboard that no one was really alone. At least, not for long. Maybe Elaina was just tuned in to the constant buzz of human activity.

Or maybe someone *was* watching her.

An elbow bumped into her stationary shoulder, and Amy jerked back, her fist automatically cocked beneath her chin.

But when she met her would-be attacker's eyes, she realized it was only Jordan and let out a quick sigh.

"Sorry about that," he muttered. "You okay?"

"I'm fine."

He opened his mouth as if he wanted to continue their endless apology dance, but she was done. Done with him. Done for the night. Done forever. So she took her excuse and ran with it. "I have to get Elaina back to her suite. I'll see you tomorrow."

He nodded, and if he tried to say anything else, it was lost as the DJ turned the bass up.

Grabbing Elaina's hand, she spun the girl toward the edge of the dance floor and the nearest exit. "It's off to bed for us," she singsonged despite Elaina's frown. But the yawn that cracked her jaw once again proved that the girl was ready for some peace and a full night of sleep, whether she'd admit it or not.

As they climbed the steps to the next level, Elaina asked, "Do you think my dad'll be there?"

"We danced for almost an hour, so I'm sure he's back from his phone call by now. And he's probably worried about you."

Elaina shook her head. "He'll know I'm with you." Suddenly the smooth skin of her face wrinkled with concern. "Will you stay with me if he's not there?"

Amy's heart tripped at the fear that laced the girl's words. Something was clearly off. Something that she couldn't quite pinpoint. But after five years with the DEA and three with the Marines before that, Amy had learned to listen to fear. She refused to let it control her, but a little healthy fear had kept her alive more than once.

"Of course. You know I'll always stay with you."

With a squeeze of her hand, Elaina rested her head against Amy's arm. "Promise?"

The plea was familiar. Probably because Amy had asked it herself a hundred times when she was about her niece's age.

But before she could respond, a wave of goose bumps rushed down her arms. Along the interior hallway there wasn't a breeze off the ocean to chill her. But something had set off her internal alarms.

"You okay, Aunt Amy?"

She whipped her head around to look behind them. The hallway was empty. "Sure." She tried to sound more certain than she felt.

There was a weight on her skin, like someone was watching them. Except they were all alone...weren't they?

And yet the sensation of being watched was as tangible as Elaina's hand in hers.

Maybe it was habit or so many years of training, but Amy grabbed the girl and pushed her into a shallow doorway, using her own body as cover. Amy measured her breaths to keep them silent, but Elaina knew no such trick. Her gasps were ragged, and they echoed in the corridor.

She couldn't identify the source of her concern, and this was the first time she'd felt this way on this cruise. But there was no doubt. Something was going on.

It had scared Elaina.

And now it was turning up every single one of Amy's protective instincts.

She peeked out from the little notch, looking both ways, but saw no one. Not even a shadow. The hallway lights had been dimmed, but there was still plenty to illuminate a moving figure.

And there was no one there.

She backed up, pulling Elaina with her and pressing the girl against her side. "Stay close."

Elaina nodded against her.

Heart thumping faster than usual, Amy took another look behind them. Maybe it would be better to backtrack. To find someone else from the wedding party.

Or she could keep going to the nearest protected place. Elaina's suite.

With slow, methodical steps she worked her way to the end of the hall, where it intersected with another. There she peeked around the corner. Two large forms were approaching and Amy jerked back, pressing Elaina against the wall behind them. Stretching a finger across her lips, she made the universal sign for quiet as heavy footsteps drew nearer.

"Where's the girl? She was supposed to be back by now."

"I don't know. I was with you. Remember?"

It sounded like the sarcastic guy got punched, and his groan echoed.

"Shut up. Don't try to be funny. I'll call the boss. He'll know where the ambassador's daughter is."

Elaina flinched, a gasp escaping. She flung a hand over her mouth and stared at Amy with wild eyes that asked the only important question. *Are they talking about me?*

Of course they were. What were the odds there was another ambassador's daughter aboard this ship?

Amy felt suddenly sick, bile rising in the back of her throat. This had gone from an instinctual concern to a serious threat in seconds. They had to get out of there, away from these men, who had clearly been watching Elaina.

"We don't know where she is. She's not back at her room yet," said the guy who'd announced he was going to call the boss.

The undeniable crackle of a walkie-talkie bounced down the hallway, but Amy couldn't understand what had been said.

"Sure. We'll get her before they arrive." Shoving his friend, he said, "Start looking."

Who was *they*? And what exactly did they want with Elaina Torres?

Whatever it was wasn't good. And Amy couldn't wait around to find out.

The deep voices dropped low, and then their footsteps stopped for a long moment before one took off in the other direction. Her heart kicked into overdrive. This was their chance to make a break for it.

Leaning down, she whispered to Elaina, "Hold my hand and don't let go."

"Are we going to find my dad?"

They were going to find safety and get help. No matter what.

TWO

Amy held Elaina's hand so tightly that their fingers shook. Or maybe that was the rest of them. Still, she pulled the girl in her wake, keeping her steps as silent and swift as possible. The halls were nearly deserted, most guests enjoying the entertainment on deck.

Her rough breathing echoed so loudly in her own head that she couldn't hear if either of the men had spotted them. And if they did, would they recognize Elaina as their mark?

"Hey!" The booming voice behind them seemed to rattle the cabin doors. "Stop!"

They'd been spotted. And apparently recognized.

Elaina slowed down, trying to look over her shoulder, pulling on Amy's arm.

"Keep running," Amy ordered. "Stay with me. Don't look back."

The little girl nodded, but her shorter legs stumbled as she tried to keep up.

There wasn't time to stop and boost Elaina onto her back, but neither could the girl's smaller feet keep up on her own. Amy pulled her close and swung her into her arms, the additional weight making every step twice as hard.

Another hallway crossed in front of them. One that would lead to the stairwell that would take them back to the deck. Then they'd be in the open. And maybe near security.

Please, God, let there be a security guard on the deck.

Feet slapping the carpet, she held every muscle in check as they approached the turn, leaning to counterbalance the weight in her arms.

"Stop right there!"

She hunched her shoulders against the anticipated gunshot, then remembered she was on a cruise ship, not in the field. She expected the possibility of being shot at on a DEA assignment. She wanted to believe that she wouldn't have to deal with that here, on the ship where no one was legally permitted to carry weapons, but she couldn't be sure.

The problem was that she didn't know what to expect here. She hadn't gotten a good look at the men talking about Elaina. There was no intel to identify their motive, their usual methods of attack or a list of their weapons.

If she'd been in the field, alone or with her

partner, she'd have looked for a strategic place to make a stand. She'd have turned and fought. She'd have disarmed first and asked questions later.

But right now there was no place to stash Elaina where she would be safe. And the girl's protection was all that mattered for the moment. Making a stand would put the girl at risk, so it wasn't an option.

As they rounded the corner, Amy caught sight of the man chasing them. She couldn't make out his features at this speed, but his wide shoulders stretched out the same black suit she'd only glimpsed before. And he charged after them, his big feet eating up the passageway as if he were an angry bull. There was something in his hand, something big and deadly stretched out in their direction.

He did have a gun.

Speed was still crucial, but she also concentrated on remembering to dodge and weave. She swooped to the left then returned to hugging the wall.

Anything to keep him off center and ensure that if he shot, his bullet would miss.

Dodge and weave.

Her mantra matched the speed of her footsteps as she flew down the hall.

They just had to keep running faster than the

man behind them until they lost him. Or found someone who could help.

But the corridor seemed to be deserted, every cabin door shut tight.

Suddenly Elaina's whole body jerked, her grip around Amy's shoulders nearly breaking as she cried loudly. Amy swallowed the scream that rose in her throat as the shift in balance nearly tripped her, forcing her to come to a momentary stop. Tears filled Elaina's eyes, and between trembling gasps she said, "My hand slipped. Sorry."

Amy dismissed the apology with a wave, hoisting the girl higher on her hip and holding on tighter. But in the moments it took to get moving again, Amy glanced back at their pursuer. He'd stopped, planting his feet shoulder-width apart and raising his gun at arm's length.

Her heart leaped to her throat, and she stumbled as she flew toward the end of the hall and a glowing red exit sign, always keeping herself between Elaina and the gun.

Please. Please. If they could just make it through that door, they might find help.

Amy crashed against the metal handle, shoving it open and tumbling against Elaina as the telltale whistle of a bullet fired through a silencer zipped toward her back.

"Go. Go. Go." She cheered herself on, forcing

herself to watch her feet and cling to the banister with her free hand.

Her shoes clanged loudly down the metal stairs. But there was no time to worry about silencing them.

That man was willing to take a shot when one of the cabin doors might have opened up at any moment. He either knew something she didn't that made him believe he wouldn't get caught, or he had nothing to lose.

Or both.

Probably both.

Her head spun as they sailed around a turn and another set of clanging footsteps joined hers.

He was gaining on them. He'd reach them long before she could get Elaina to safety.

Dear God, help us. It was the only prayer she could manage as her heart kept up a steady tattoo. *Go. Go. Go.*

And then another whistle, so high-pitched that she felt rather than heard it, sailed past. The shot splintered the corner of the door frame as they barreled through it. Elaina screamed.

Good. She could scream all she wanted now. Anything to gain some attention.

But the deck was empty, and the sound was lost on the wind as they rushed into the open.

Where was everyone? Had the entire ship migrated to the lido deck for more fun with Neesha and Rodney?

She whipped around to see how close their pursuer was. The clanging of his feet against the metal steps gave him away. He wasn't visible yet, but he was closing in. And she couldn't risk leading him to the party. There were too many innocent lives there. People she loved. But she and Elaina were sitting ducks out here.

Where to go? Where would they be safe?

Out of the corner of her eye, she saw the closed door of what looked like a small storage closet. But as she turned toward it, she ran directly into an unmoving chest.

Large hands clamped on both of her shoulders, surrounding Elaina and stopping her midstep. "Amy? Are you all right? I thought I heard someone screaming."

She had to peer all the way up into his face to get a good look at Jordan, but even then her eyes wouldn't quite focus on him. Her shoulders twitched as she tried to check behind her.

"Amy." His tone was clipped, his eyes darting from her to Elaina and back. "What's wrong?"

Everything in her melted. She hadn't even known she'd wanted his help, but now that he was here, she recognized him as exactly what they needed. "Someone's chasing us. Shot at us." Her words came out on a pant, but she flung her finger out behind her and met his gaze for a brief second.

If he needed to think through his actions, it took him only a fragment of a second. He grabbed them both, shifting them out of the line of view of the stairwell. "Stay right here. Don't move."

And then he ran toward the doorway. But instead of going into the stairwell, he slipped to the side, his back against the white outer wall, his ear pressed in.

She took a step to follow him, but stopped as Elaina let out a small sob. "It's okay, honey," she said, cuddling her niece close. Everything inside her cried out to help Jordan take care of this guy, but she couldn't possibly carry Elaina into that kind of situation, and leaving her behind was equally impossible, so she held her position with watchful eyes.

Their pursuer had reached the bottom of the stairs, and the pace of his clanging steps had slowed.

But it didn't calm the tantrum of her heart. Or loosen the way Elaina's skinny arms squeezed around her neck. Pressing Elaina's face against her shoulder, Amy tried to hold her tight enough to keep both of them from falling apart.

But she couldn't look away from Jordan, whose shoulders rose and fell in a steady rhythm.

His face was a mask of calm, and he closed his eyes for a long second.

She wanted to scream at him, to tell him to pay attention. He was going to miss it all, and she and Elaina would be easy pickings for their pursuer. But she bit her lips until they stung and she tasted the coppery tang of blood.

And suddenly the entire world seemed to explode. Everything happened at once. A wicked Glock 23—silencer attached—came through the entrance, their pursuer holding it straight out and ready to fire. But before the rest of him could make it through the doorway, Jordan squeezed his hands together, raised them over his head and brought both of his arms down on top of the other man's. There was a sickening crack, and the gun flew across the deck as the man groaned and swore. But before he could do anything more, Jordan landed an elbow to his sternum.

The man in black crumpled to the floor.

Years of training told Amy to secure the weapon, but when she tried to put Elaina down so she could grab the gun, Elaina whimpered and refused to let go. So she took her with, racing for the gun, scooping it up and pointing it at the still man on the ground.

"Are you all right?" Jordan asked, his hands swiftly moving up and down the beefy arms and legs of their pursuer, searching for additional weapons. Suddenly he stopped and stared hard at her. The gentleness he'd displayed with his cousin earlier in the evening was gone. Replaced by something that could only be called his mission face. It was all hard angles and firm planes. The teasing smile that he so often used had disappeared. Even the little cleft in his chin seemed especially dark.

And she was so busy studying his face that she nearly missed his repeated question. "Amy, are you all right? Were you hurt?"

"What? No. We're fine. You're fine, right Elaina?" The girl nodded despite the persistent trembling of her chin.

Amy's own adrenaline was dropping fast and making her hands shake, but she held on to her niece and kept going. "A little shaken up, but we're all right. Who is this guy?" Her words came out on a rush, but they seemed to be all Jordan needed before going back to work, confirming she had scooped up the only weapon.

When he was satisfied, Jordan pulled the man's arms behind his back, which launched a loud groan.

"Might have cracked a bone there," Jordan said. As apologies went, it wasn't much. But somehow she didn't think he spent much time telling bad guys he was sorry.

And that was just fine with her.

"Go find an officer or security guard and bring them back here."

"But there was another man, too. He went the other way, but they were talking. What if he comes to see what's keeping his friend?"

He looked into the silent stairwell, but shook his head. "If he shows up, I'll handle it. The two of you go now."

His blunt orders made her hackles stand on end, but she fought the urge to tell him she could take care of it. She could. Usually. In any other circumstance.

But she was responsible for Elaina. And she'd rather die than leave the girl open and vulnerable to another attack.

Jordan was skilled and experienced. And no matter how much she hated admitting it—especially to herself—there were few people she trusted to handle an unexpected threat more.

When she found a security officer, it took a bit of convincing to get him to follow her back to the scene. But the gun in her hand, which she'd emptied of bullets, piqued his curiosity.

"Guns aren't allowed on the ship." He looked equal parts confused and angry, his pasty cheeks going red and splotchy.

"I know." She'd left hers at home, locked in her gun safe. And it was a fair guess that Jordan had done the same. Amy felt a little bare without her weapon, and she wondered if Jordan felt the same way. Either he felt as unprotected as the day he was born or he didn't even notice because he was fully equipped to use his hands to neutralize any threat.

Downed man in a black suit was exhibit A.

For the moment, they had no idea how the man had gotten a gun on board. But that would have to wait. "We need to see the captain."

The guard agreed, and followed her and Elaina back to Jordan, who stood over their pursuer like a hunter showing off his haul.

As the trio approached, the guard let out an audible gasp, and she tried to look at Jordan through his eyes, to consider what it would be like to see him for the first time. He'd been a part of her life for almost as long as she'd been friends with Neesha—more than twenty years. So the big shoulders and towering height didn't frighten her. The size of his biceps and strength in his grip didn't intimidate her. No, they made her feel...

Well, it was better not to think about how they made her feel.

After more than sixteen years of daydreaming about how he made her feel, she'd realized just how wrong she'd been.

It was better for her—better for everyone—if she just moved on.

Only she couldn't deny that, in this moment, he made her feel safe. And she'd never been more grateful.

The big guy in the black suit groaned again, his head lolling to the side as the officer cuffed him. It took both Jordan and the comparatively puny guard to drag the man upright. And it seemed to take hours to make it across the ship and down three levels to the security office. They'd gotten a few strange looks, but most of the ship's guests were too wrapped up in their own vacation to give more than a passing glance to a man leaning on a security guard and another man, who could have been his friend.

When they finally arrived, Amy sank into a chair, Elaina by her side. As she wrapped an arm around her niece, she whispered to a nearby security guard, "Can you get her father down here? He was in the captain's office not too long ago."

The guard nodded, and Amy squeezed her hands together in her lap to keep them from trembling.

His hands were still shaking.

Jordan tried to hold them still, but there wasn't much he could do to stop the adrenaline charging through him. What kept him on his feet during a confrontation always left him feeling a little out of sorts when the conflict was resolved.

But as he stared through the window into the makeshift cell at the unconscious man, and then looked back at Amy, he could do little more than thank God that he'd heard Elaina's screams and gone to investigate. There was no telling what the man would have done when he'd caught them. But while Jordan was glad he'd been able to protect Amy and Elaina, he needed more information if he was going to be able to continue keeping them safe. Question number one: Why had the man been chasing them?

And as much as he wanted to beg for answers, Elaina's stricken face left him mute. She'd have to rehash the whole ordeal when the captain arrived, so he'd patiently wait for that.

Well, *patiently* was a subjective word.

He paced the confines of the little room. The security guard manning the office, who had identified himself as Paul Cortero, had called Michael Torres and then leaned back in his big black chair, his hands resting over his stomach. He didn't look terribly disturbed or concerned that a man carrying a heavy-duty handgun with a silencer had just attacked a woman and an eight-year-old girl. In fact, his eyes were closed as he rocked in his seat.

Incompetent fool.

Those were the kindest words Jordan had for a man like Cortero, who showed so little concern for the people whose safety was in his care.

But calling him every name in the book wasn't going to locate the other man Amy had mentioned or resolve this issue.

So he kept on marching because movement helped him think.

Suddenly the metal door flew open, and a short, thin man barreled into the room, followed by a much larger shadow of a guard. Michael Torres usually had a big, commanding presence, despite being several inches shy of six feet. But right now his eyes were filled with panic as he surveyed the room.

Elaina jumped from her chair and flung herself into her father's arms. "I was so scared, Daddy. He was chasing us, and he said he had to find me." The words were muffled, but the terror in them was real.

"It's okay, honey. It's going to be okay."

Except a gnawing feeling in his stomach told Jordan that they couldn't be so sure of that. This situation wasn't something they could control. At least not yet. Not with at least one more man out there.

When Elaina pulled back with tearstained cheeks, she grasped for Amy's arm. "Aunt Amy was so great. She saved me."

Torres hugged his sister-in-law and mouthed a thank-you.

She nodded, but there was no accompanying smile. And a tick at the corner of her eye suggested that she had news. News that no one was going to want to hear.

And Jordan was entirely sure it had to do with what Elaina had just said. The man chasing them had been after the little girl.

His stomach took a nosedive, but before he could analyze the situation further, Torres turned toward him.

"Somerton." He gave a curt nod, his eyebrows pulled together. "How did you get involved in this?"

Jordan cringed, wishing he'd had a second to remind Torres that, as far as the rest of the world was concerned, they'd had no reason to ever meet.

Amy cut in, "Wait. How do you know each other?"

Torres turned back to Amy but was spared finding an explanation when the door to the office opened again and the captain marched in. His white jacket shone under the sterile lights as he reached to shake the ambassador's hand.

"I wasn't expecting to see you again tonight."

"I wasn't, either." Torres's face was pinched as he looked down at Elaina, her arms still wrapped around his waist. "It seems my daughter and her aunt ran into some trouble outside our cabin tonight."

The captain motioned toward the chairs to indicate they should sit down while Cortero scrambled to give his seat to the ship's senior officer.

As the captain introduced himself, Jordan forced himself to stop pacing and slid into the chair beside Amy, who shot him a look that said she wasn't going to let her question drop.

"I'm Captain Robertson." He directed his introduction to Elaina, who was perched on her father's leg. He barely looked at Jordan and Amy and ignored Torres's bodyguard standing in the corner. "I heard you had quite an evening. Can you tell me about it?"

Elaina nodded, her dark hair slipping over her shoulders. "I was with Aunt Amy. We were at the party for Neesha."

"And then what happened?"

She looked at Amy, who gave her a gentle smile, before continuing. "We were almost to my room, and then we heard some men. They were talking. About me. Said they had to find me. Aunt Amy and I tried to get away but one of them followed us. He yelled for us to stop, but we didn't. Then there was a high-pitched whistling sound. It was weird, but we got to the stairs."

Even though he'd seen the gun, Jordan cringed as Elaina gave her trembling account of being shot at. It didn't sound like she even knew what that whistle had been, but he did. And it was enough to make him sick.

Two thugs looking for a little girl when her father and his bodyguard were away from the room. Armed and dangerous and willing to use violence to get their way.

That wasn't coincidence.

"How do you know they were looking for you specifically?" Robertson asked.

Amy filled in the gaps Elaina had left. "The two men were talking loud enough that we could hear them from around the corner." She met Jordan's gaze and held it, the anxiety there present and accounted for. "One asked the other where 'the girl' was. They called her the ambassador's daughter." Amy nodded toward Torres. "When they didn't find her, they radioed someone they called 'the boss.' Then they split up and one headed right for us, so we made a run for it."

Leaning forward, Jordan tried to put the

scene together in his mind's eye. "Did they say anything else? Or indicate who was in charge?"

Amy chewed on her lower lip, turning it pink and plump. But it was Elaina who added, "The man said they had to have me before *they* arrive."

Jordan sucked in a sharp breath but held it because he couldn't risk cutting her off if there was more to the story.

Torres didn't hesitate. "They? Who's they?"

"He never said." Amy wrapped her arms around her stomach, as though she could ward off the chill from this conversation.

But Jordan was lost somewhere in the simple words Elaina had repeated. Everyone else had focused on the *who*. But he was stumped on the *how*. His forehead puckering as he tried to work it out, he wondered if maybe the girl had simply gotten the words wrong. "Arrive? They said *arrive*?"

Amy's deep brown doe eyes grew even larger, and he could tell the emphasis hadn't been lost on her. "Yes. That's exactly what he said."

"How exactly does someone *arrive* on a cruise ship in the middle of the ocean?"

THREE

No matter how many ways Jordan flipped the questions over in his mind, there was no answer for them and no rhyme or reason to what the men had said—or what they'd tried to do.

Someone had attempted to kidnap the daughter of the ambassador to Lybania. On a cruise ship. In the middle of the Caribbean. But why try to abduct the girl on a ship where there were a finite number of places to hide her once they captured her? Why choose a ship with equally limited ways for them to escape from the people who would be searching for Elaina until they pulled into port? They weren't even scheduled to arrive in St. Thomas for two more days.

Even more puzzling was the imminent arrival of the illusive *they*. He had no idea who that could be. And even less where or when their arrival might take place. The arrival that had been mentioned would have to come by helicopter or boat. But either would draw significant attention. Is that what they wanted?

His only clue was *soon*. Because the men Amy had overheard had been in a rush to get their hands on Elaina.

But that left a whole lot of holes in his intel.

What he needed was information from the man in the black suit, who had finally begun to wake up and was holding his arm like he'd received a lethal blow. Bah. It had barely been a tap. Just enough to bring him down. If he didn't like it, well, then he shouldn't shoot at women and children.

Which brought Jordan right back to another question. How'd he get a gun on board the ship? Had he snuck it through security? Had it been stashed in his suite waiting for him? And why would he shoot at Elaina if his goal was to kidnap her?

The questions pounded like a woodpecker against steel. He was getting exactly nowhere.

No matter how long he paced, the walls of the security office were as confining as the unanswered questions in his mind.

Amy, too, had stood when the captain excused himself for an urgent call. But Elaina slumped in her father's lap. "Can we go back to our room now?" she mumbled against his chest.

"No!"

Torres jumped as Jordan, Amy and the bodyguard all yelled the same word at the same time. But the ambassador's eyes were knowing, even as Amy slipped into the seat she'd just vacated to rub Elaina's back. "We'll get you a new room." *A safe one.*

The last line was unspoken but louder than her other words.

Suddenly the door swung open and the captain and another man in a starched white jacket—the second in command—entered.

"My apologies," the captain said. "This is Julio Xavier, my staff captain."

Jordan shook Xavier's hand but skipped the pleasantries. "The ambassador, his daughter and their bodyguard need to be moved to a new suite right away."

Captain Robertson nodded and motioned to Torres, who stood, still holding Elaina. "I'll take care of it personally. Follow me." Just before he slipped out of the office with Torres and Elaina, and their bodyguard following closely, he turned back to Jordan. "Xavier oversees security and is in charge of our prisoner."

Jordan nodded but addressed Amy instead of the staff captain. "It's been a long night. You should get some rest."

Her lips pinched at his words, and she pressed flat hands together in front of her so hard that her arms shook. He could almost see the steam coming from her ears.

She was clearly exhausted, and he'd assumed that she'd be grateful for the chance to get some downtime, knowing he'd handle things here. Apparently not.

He scratched at the back of his neck and frowned at Amy, who gave him one shake of her head before turning toward Xavier and pointing toward the glass window into the single cell.

"With your permission, sir, I'd like to interview this man."

Jordan stepped forward to interrupt. After all, he wanted to do the interrogating.

But Xavier was focused on Amy, shaking his head at her. "It's my jurisdiction. I'll take care of it."

"Sir, I'm a DEA agent and that little girl's aunt. And that man shot at me today. I'd like to know why."

The staff captain ran his hand along his jaw, pinching his features as though in deep thought before letting his gaze land on Jordan. "Suppose you're DEA, too."

"No, sir."

Xavier visibly relaxed.

"SEAL teams."

The older man's pinched expression immediately returned. "SEALs, huh? So you've worked with terrorists before."

Jordan wasn't quite sure where this line of questioning was going, but he'd answer nearly any question to get a chance at asking a few of his own. "No, sir. I don't work *with* terrorists."

"Ha." Xavier's chuckle was as dry as dust.

"What do you say you let us stick around?" Jordan said. "We'll stay out of your way."

Amy cleared her throat as if she wasn't willing to make that concession, but Jordan kept going.

"Maybe ask a follow-up question or two."

Xavier rubbed at his chin for a long moment before glancing at Cortero, who had remained silent in the background. "I guess that's fine."

As jails went, this one looked more like a hospital, all sterile white walls and a bench that looked like it belonged in an accessible shower. It wasn't exactly homey, but neither did it suggest that the man in the black suit would face serious consequences for his actions. Which left Jordan with a distinct feeling of unbalance.

Xavier began his interview in a calm voice. "I'm Julio Xavier. What's your name?"

The thug shook his head. He attempted to cross his arms but winced when he bumped his forearm. "I need to see a doctor. That guy broke my arm."

Amy shot Jordan a look, and he shrugged. He'd take the man—or any other—down again in a minute if he threatened Amy or Elaina.

Xavier sucked on his long tooth. "First, you have to tell me your name."

The big man squinted hard, his eyes nearly disappearing in his round face. His bald head didn't do anything except make his face look fatter.

After a long staring contest, where the staff captain didn't back down, the man said, "Dean."

"Is that a first name or a last?"

Again, he stared like he was trying to figure out what Xavier wanted to hear. Jordan couldn't stop his hands from rubbing together or force his feet to stand still. Not when there was another man out there, probably still looking for Elaina, and this man in front of him was answering none of the questions burning a hole in Jordan's gut.

Maybe it was a good thing he wasn't doing the questioning because Jordan suddenly had patience for no one and nothing.

Come on, man. Get it going.

But the staff captain kept his pace slow and easy. "Is your first name Dean?"

The man shook his head.

"Your last?"

Finally a nod. Now they were getting somewhere. Mr. Dean had half a name, and Xavier nodded to Cortero. "Look it up."

The security guard did as he was told, turning to the computer on the desk before him, his fingers making the keyboard clack. "First name?"

The man in black responded with silence, long enough to make Jordan's blood begin to boil. He shot a scowl into the cell, but it was Amy who spoke up.

"Now."

One word. One syllable. It was all she needed. "Eric. Eric Dean."

Jordan couldn't contain the smile that bubbled into place, and he shot Amy an approving nod as Cortero typed in the first name.

"There's no one by that name on the passenger manifest."

Amy drew in a quick breath. He could feel it more than hear it. And he was pretty sure they were thinking the same thing.

This man had either lied about his name or found a back door onto the ship. With a gun.

And he wasn't alone. There was at least one other dangerous person working with him, and they were both working for someone else. But if there *was* a back entrance, there could be a whole lot more than that.

"We're going to need your fingerprints to confirm your identity," Xavier said.

But Eric shook his head. Hard. He looked like a five-year-old refusing to go to bed. "I'll wait to see the doctor first. And then I'll wait for the local authorities in St. Thomas."

His words were straightforward and clear, but something about his expression made Jordan's skin crawl. He wasn't scared or upset, or even resigned to his fate. He seemed to be suppressing a smile at the thought that he'd ever have to face the consequences of his actions. Either he was a sociopath or he knew something that Jordan didn't.

Jordan guessed that when it came to this situation, there were a lot of things he didn't know.

And that didn't sit well with him.

Turning to Amy, he frowned, trying to figure out how to convince her that pressing Dean for answers was a dead end. But she beat him to it.

"We're not going to get anything out of him tonight," she said. Then she looked right at Xavier. "Will you call me if he gets talkative?"

He nodded, and she strode toward the exit. As she walked out into the hallway, Jordan waved at Xavier and chased her down. "Hey, where do you think you're going?"

Amy didn't have the energy left to fight with Jordan about where she was going or why. In fact, all she really wanted to do was crash in her bed and sleep until this night was nothing but a bad dream.

But that wasn't an option.

So she stopped and put her hands on her hips, looking way up into his face. "I'm going to talk with Michael. Because whoever this Dean guy is, he was serious about finding Elaina. If someone's after her, it's got to be because of Michael. And anyone with the audacity to try to kidnap an ambassador's daughter isn't going to stop after one failed attempt."

Her stomach clenched as she spoke the words aloud.

It was one thing to know they were true. Another entirely to speak them.

Jordan didn't look surprised in the least, and his brown eyes only turned darker. "Then I guess we better find their new room."

He said it casually, as though they were stuck together, and she couldn't help but blurt out the truth. "You can go, you know. Get some rest. It's late. It's been a long night, and this isn't your problem. I'll be fine."

He shrugged, not bothering to reply to her dismissal. "Let's swing by the captain's office to get their new suite number."

She frowned but didn't have any choice except to follow him, racing to keep up with his long strides.

"I'll handle it. She's my responsibility."

His eyebrows bunched together as he stared at her. "What about her dad? Isn't she *his* responsibility?"

Amy's chest tightened, her hands drawing into fists. How could she possibly explain that while she loved her brother-in-law and understood that he had an important job, lately he'd been breaking promises to his daughter and missing family dinners. She knew he cared deeply for Elaina, but he was neglecting her, all the same. Maybe Amy saw it because she knew the signs. Because she'd lived through it. But she wasn't eager to parade the pain of her own childhood, so she squared her shoulders and clarified, "She's my niece. And I won't let anything happen to her."

Jordan stopped short, and she nearly bumped into him. He faced her and bent until they were practically nose-to-nose. "Neither will I."

And as though that closed the door on any argument, he began walking again. She had to run to catch up. But there was a piece of her—infinitely small—that smiled at his announcement. She'd rather have a partner in this than not. Jordan wasn't the partner she'd have chosen—but when it came to her niece's safety, she'd take any help she could get.

In no time at all they reached the captain's

office, received Michael's new suite number and arrived at the cabin. Jordan lifted his hand to thump the side of his fist against the white wood, but Amy grabbed his forearm before he could connect.

"What are you doing?"

The lines around his mouth deepened, his eyebrows angling down. "What do you mean? I'm knocking." He spoke like she was a child, and she glared back at him, wishing he wasn't quite so much taller than she was.

"Elaina might have fallen asleep. So maybe don't wake her up and scare her socks off by pounding on the door in the middle of the night."

With a frown and a shake of his head, he stepped back and waved his hand in front of the door. "By all means. Show me how it's done."

Oh, she could show him a thing or two.

And she would…if Elaina wasn't in jeopardy and there wasn't at least one thug still free on this ship.

Rolling her eyes at him, she gently rapped on the door with the edge of her knuckles. *Bump-bump-buh-buh-bump. Bump. Bump.*

The door quickly opened, and Jordan whispered in her ear as Michael led them into the suite, "No fair. You didn't tell me there was a secret knock."

"You didn't ask."

"Hmm?" Michael looked up, his eyes wild and dark hair thoroughly disheveled as though he'd been running his fingers through it all night. He probably had. "Did you say something?"

"No." Amy gave the room a quick visual sweep, taking in Pete standing beside the closed door on the far side of the room. That had to be Elaina's room, and it was clear that Michael's bodyguard wasn't going to let a soul past. That, at least, unwound one string from around her lungs.

Michael's restless marching threatened to tie it right back up.

"Can I get you something to drink?" she asked, shooting a quick glance toward the kitchenette to her left. It had a not-quite-full-size refrigerator tucked between two lengths of Formica countertop. Each slab was bare save for a coffeemaker that could make only one cup at a time. "Water? Tea? Decaf?"

Michael's eyes were trained on the floor, and when he looked up again, they narrowed in confusion. "What?"

She glanced at Jordan, whose eyes mirrored the concern she felt. With a gentle sweep of his hands, he encouraged her to keep going.

She lowered herself to the edge of the chocolate-brown sofa. "Michael, why don't you sit down with me for a minute? Talk to me. Tell me what you're thinking." Keeping her voice low and even, she managed a half smile, which didn't garner any reaction from her brother-in-law.

"Michael, what happened tonight?"

He stopped pacing, slammed one hand on his hip and stabbed the other through his hair. "You were there. You're the one who told me."

Taking a deep breath through her nose, she let it out through tight lips, trying to formulate a line of questioning that would lead to answers.

She needed to know what he knew. And she needed that info now.

But she was going to have to guide him there.

Jordan cleared his throat from across the room. He'd taken up a chunk of space outside the kitchen area, leaning a shoulder against the wall. His arms were crossed over his chest but the relaxed angle of his neck made him seem… what? She couldn't quite put her finger on it.

At ease, maybe.

And somehow it helped her breathe just a little easier.

Maybe Michael picked up on that, too. He took a step, then paused. Then he sank into an overstuffed armchair.

"The man in the cell tonight," Jordan began slowly, thoughtfully, "have you ever seen him before?"

Shoulders slumping until his arms rested on his knees, Michael shook his head. "No."

Jordan kept his voice low and easy. "Had Elaina ever seen him before?"

"I don't think so. No. I'm pretty sure she hadn't."

Jordan scratched at his chin, his gaze going to the ceiling like he was formulating his next question. "Do you usually go on vacation with a bodyguard?"

The question made both Amy and Michael snap to attention, and she stared at Jordan.

"I'm just saying," Jordan continued, "Lybania's a high-risk area, so I'm sure you're provided with a protection detail when you're at the embassy or traveling in Lybania. But I don't know very many ambassadors who vacation on US soil with a bodyguard."

"We're not on US soil," Michael said.

Jordan uncrossed and recrossed his arms, his gaze never wavering. Silence lingered too long and too heavy to last.

Even the silent bodyguard in question shifted from one foot to the other.

Finally Michael put his hands over his face and sighed.

"I think someone is trying to kill me. And now they're coming after Elaina."

FOUR

Now they're coming after Elaina.

The words rolled around Amy's head and filled her with dread.

She shifted on the couch, stretching all five feet and nine inches of herself across the cushions to try to relieve the pressure at the back of her throat. It didn't help. Neither did closing her eyes.

The truth remained.

And, with it, the fear.

She knew about fighting and facing down the ugliest that the world had to offer. Her experience in the DEA had shown her the worst of what people were capable of doing to one another.

But in those scenarios, the ones needing to be rescued were faceless and often nameless. Their rescue was a mission, an order. She went in because it was her job. She cared about doing it well and gave her all to making the world a safer place, but at the end of the day, it was still just a job. It had nothing to do with her family.

But Elaina as the target of a kidnapping and maybe attempted murder? This was personal. Amy would protect her niece at all costs.

No matter what Jordan said.

And he'd had plenty to say while Michael had explained what he'd meant about the danger he and his daughter were in.

There had been death threats at his office in Washington. Letters mostly. But then there was a bomb scare. The DC police department hadn't found any sign of an explosive, but it was obvious that Michael had been spooked even as he tried to brush them off as extremists. Of course, the threats in Lybania didn't come in the form of letters or phone calls. There were no warnings, just attacks. He expected that in the field. But in the States? Not so much.

"The Department of Foreign Services officers said it might be good for me to get out of town for a while so they could investigate." Michael had looked up at her with pleading eyes like a basset hound, begging her to understand. "I probably should have told you, but I'd hoped it wouldn't be necessary. I thought we'd be safe on a cruise. I mean, we're in the middle of the ocean, right? And that's why I only brought

Pete. I figured one guy wouldn't stand out too much in a crowd, and he'd get the job done."

The bodyguard had stood silently as Michael laid out everything he knew. And when it was his turn, Pete corroborated the story. "We didn't see any indication that there would be trouble here on the cruise."

The room fell into silence until Jordan eventually spoke. "Any idea who's behind the threats?"

Michael hunched his shoulders, leaned on his knees and shook his head. "The DFS is running through a list of possibilities, but given the tensions in Lybania, it's a challenge to narrow things down, especially since we aren't sure of their agenda. There haven't been any demands made." He rubbed his hands together, keeping his head low. "It's not unheard of for threats to be made against ambassadors, but since the assassination…" Then he looked up, staring pointedly at Jordan.

Amy stared at Jordan, too, waiting for a reaction. But there was no movement of his features, least of all the furrowed brow of confusion.

Her chest clenched.

A little over a year ago, a high-profile Lybanian terrorist had been killed. Shot by a sniper at five hundred yards.

And, as far as she knew, no one had ever taken credit for it. Right along with the rest of the world, she'd assumed that the Lybanian government had taken him out to destabilize the terrorist group.

But that look in Michael's eyes, directed at Jordan…it was knowing. Concerning.

"Have things in Lybania been unsettled since then?" she asked.

Michael shrugged. "It's hard to say. How do you compare mayhem to mayhem? The terrorists are fearless, and they have been for years. You know about those aid workers who were kidnapped a few years back—taken in broad daylight."

Jordan and Amy nodded. One of their mutual friends had been a relief worker rescued from the Lybanian terrorists by Jordan's SEAL team.

"The factions are growing—it feels like there are new terrorist cells every day." Michael sighed. "I thought the assassination might bring some peace to the region. And it did. For about a week. Now everyone is clamoring for power. Some seem to want American aid. Others just want us out of the Middle East altogether."

Jordan caught her eye with a tick of his head. His look spoke volumes, spelling out all the same concerns that she had and adding a gut punch to go with them.

They were most likely dealing with Lybanian terrorists who had tracked the ambassador to the cruise ship and sought to strike against him while he was relatively unprotected. But exactly what faction they represented and what they wanted—beyond Elaina—wasn't clear.

Which made the terrorists even more dangerous.

If she knew what they wanted, she could try to get it for them. Or at least *act* like she was getting it for them until backup arrived.

But first they had to get backup on its way.

Jordan beat her to the question. "Have you been in touch with Washington tonight? Do they know what's happening?"

Michael's eyes grew to twice their normal size. "No." His hands fluttered and his voice rose as he pointed toward the door beyond Pete. "I was too busy taking care of Elaina."

Jordan's hand gesture was low, nonconfrontational. "It's okay. But we need to let them know right away. They can send the Coast Guard or get some help from the port at St. Thomas." It was less suggestion and more order. And Amy was glad it had come from the SEAL. Even though she'd been thinking the same thing, her brother-in-law could more easily ignore her, thinking she was overreacting. She was practically a little sister to him.

But there was something unyielding about Jordan that demanded a response.

Michael jumped to his feet, his gaze traveling to Pete and then back to Jordan. "I should. Yes. That's right. I'll make the call right now." He picked up the corded phone sitting on the end table beside the couch and punched in a quick code. "This is Ambassador Torres. Tell the captain I'm on my way to see him. I need to use his secure phone line." There was a long pause. "When did they call? They're still on the line?" He hung up without any warning and marched toward the door.

"My office just called for me. The captain's assistant was just dialing me right now. They're waiting on the line. I've got to go take this." With a hand on the doorknob, Michael said, "I'll be back soon."

But Pete marched toward him, then stopped short. "You're not going alone, sir." His gaze darted toward the bedroom door, the war with him clearly visible. He couldn't be in two places at once.

Michael held up his hand. "Stay with Elaina. I'll be fine."

Pete's eyebrows formed a deep V, and he crossed his arms. "I don't think—"

Amy stood. "I'll stay with Elaina. You and Pete go. Just make sure that someone in Washington knows what's going on. Even if they can't get here right away, they can still do some digging for us, and maybe figure out who we're dealing with. Any new information could help."

Pete's stance relaxed, and he nodded. But Michael wasn't quite so sure. His grip on the door handle tightened until his knuckles turned white.

"I'll stay, too." Again, Jordan's tone implied a decided course of action rather than a suggestion. And while she'd appreciated it earlier, this time it made her hackles stand up.

"We'll be fine." The words came out sounding just as confident as she felt. Which wasn't quite as confident as she'd like. Especially when Jordan's eyes narrowed another fraction of an inch. He seemed to be questioning her abilities without saying a word.

And that wasn't fair. She was trained and fully capable. And, yes, a little tired. But that wasn't going to keep her from protecting Elaina.

She squared her shoulders and spoke to Michael, but her gaze remained on Jordan. "Go now. You'll be there and back before anyone has any idea that you were even gone."

Jordan gave a quick nod, and Michael and Pete disappeared with the quiet snick of the closing door. But Jordan remained. And even though he was silent, just knowing he was so close by scraped at her nerves.

Maybe it was her God-given independence.

Perhaps it was her competitive nature wanting to prove her own abilities. It could be the way his very presence reminded her of her most embarrassing moment.

Her insides did a full flip. This was neither the time nor the place to think about how he'd made her a laughingstock in front of his whole family. Taking a deep breath, she pressed her hands together and tried to form an argument that would give her a moment's reprieve from his presence.

Suddenly it was there.

"What about Neesha? Do you think someone should check on her? If Dean and his partner know about Elaina, they might know she's part of a bridal party."

His posture whipped to attention, and she couldn't hold back a smug smile. She'd thought of something he hadn't.

"Right. Yeah, someone should make sure the rest of the family hasn't been targeted to get to Elaina." He pulled his cell phone from his pocket and waved it at her. "Call me if there's even a hint of trouble."

"I can't call your cell."

He looked at his phone like it had betrayed him, rather than being hobbled through a lack of cell towers on the ship. "Fine. Text me, then."

They'd all paid for the Wi-Fi service while

on board—and it would cover their texting, too. "All right."

He stepped toward the door, but turned back toward her. "Be careful, okay? Stay alert."

She wasn't a rookie. And she almost told him so, but he interrupted her.

"There are a lot of people on this ship who care about you." He turned away but spun back before adding almost as an afterthought. "And Elaina."

After she locked the door that he shut behind him, Amy let out a soft sigh and looked around the suite. It was furnished in the same muted colors as her own cabin. Only this one had three times as much space—and that was just in the living area. Two couches faced each other, and she checked behind each. Then she opened every interior door. The closets were empty save for the standard ironing board and hotel hangers. The kitchen pantry contained a small basket of pre-stocked food items.

Everything was in its place.

Which didn't account for the nagging sense of unease that was tingling at the top of her spine. But since she saw nothing out of place, she had to believe she was just being paranoid.

So she had laid down on the sofa and stared at the ceiling, waiting for Michael's return. Fifteen. Twenty. Thirty minutes passed.

But the low buzz of anticipation still hummed through her, and she pushed herself to her feet, wandering the room and checking the locks again.

She moved to Elaina's door and pressed her ear to the center. All was silent on the other side, so she turned the handle and opened it a crack. Elaina lay in the center of a queen bed, her arms stretched out to each side and her dark hair wild across her white pillow.

Suddenly a bump against the exterior door made her jump. It was soft, almost like someone had tried to muffle the sound.

She held her breath and waited.

Lord, let that be the creaking of the ship.

Something bumped again.

And the door handle gave a gentle jiggle.

Heart suddenly hammering in her throat, Amy ran for the door, peeked through the peephole and nearly swallowed her tongue. A giant black shoulder hunched in her view, the man's face turned away. She wanted to scream, but discipline held the noise in. He was clearly working on the electronic keypad as another shadow fell across the hallway behind him.

The dull thrumming of the ship dissolved until all she could hear was the rushing of blood through her ears.

They were back. They were coming for Elaina.

And Amy was the only person standing between them and the little girl.

Racing across the living room, she reached the far side of a sofa and shoved at its end. It didn't even budge. She leaned against the armrest with her shoulder and gave another hard push. Nothing.

The furniture was probably bolted down in case of severe waves.

She huffed and spun around, searching for anything that might not be screwed to the floor that she could use to barricade the door. The four chairs around the dining room table looked too flimsy to hold the door in place, and the wooden credenza along the far wall didn't even tried to hide the bolts holding it in place.

She gave another frantic spin. Made another desperate search.

Finally her gaze landed on the mahogany coffee table between the couches. Its legs were ornately curved, but the rectangular top was solid and nearly two inches thick.

Dragging it across the carpet, she stumbled, lost her grip and fell hard on her rear end. But she wasn't getting points for style.

All that mattered was Elaina and her safety.

After several attempts, she got the table into

place and shoved it beneath the door handle. It sat at a good angle, but it wouldn't keep the men out indefinitely.

And then what? Then she'd have to face them. At least two of them. Maybe more.

She'd fight for that little girl until she died.

But then what would happen to Elaina?

She couldn't even consider it, so she gave the table another shove, smacking the wood against the metal handle of the door. The crack must have alerted the men on the other side, as they dropped any pretense of subtlety. A shoulder or foot slammed into the door without preamble.

She needed help. Fast.

She ran across the room and snatched up the receiver for the suite's phone. It was dead. No dial tone. Nothing. It had been working thirty minutes ago, so they must have cut the phone lines. Maybe the ones between all of the rooms. Maybe just this room. It didn't matter.

These men knew that Elaina had been moved to a new suite. And they'd cut her new room off from the rest of the ship.

Except for maybe Wi-Fi.

She yanked her cell out of her pocket. There was only one person she could think to text, so she whipped a message out to him.

They're back.

At the crack of the splintering door frame, she nearly dropped her phone. But the metal security lock was still in place and its rattle filled the room right along with the grumbles of one of the men on the other side. He cursed long and low in a language that was both foreign and somehow familiar.

As she sprinted toward the bedroom door, her phone buzzed in her hand.

Hide. Now. On my way.

She could almost hear the growl of Jordan's voice.

With each step she took, the lock rattled. The table shook. She flinched.

And getting to Elaina wasn't going to save her. Not if these men were armed.

"Break it down." The heavy accent couldn't disguise the man's sinister intent.

"I'm trying," his comrade said.

Just as her hand reached the cool knob of Elaina's room, wood fractured and Amy dove into the bedroom.

"Aunt Amy?" Elaina sat up in bed, rubbing her eyes. "What's happening?"

"Shh." Pressing one finger to her lips, she scooped the little girl up with her other arm and whisked her toward the closet. "We have to be very, very quiet."

"But—"

Amy pressed her hand over Elaina's mouth briefly and shook her head hard. She mouthed the word *quiet* and prayed that her niece would understand, even in the darkness that covered the room.

Elaina squirmed in her lap as Amy squatted inside the confines of the closet, peering through the wooden slats into the blackness of the room. For a moment the only sounds were Elaina's strangled breaths and fidgets and rustling.

Then came a grunt and something that sounded like a copper pot being ripped in half. The security lock had been breached.

Where are you?

Her phone lit up, bright enough to illuminate Elaina's wide eyes and quivering lips, and Amy hated the fact that she'd been forced to leave her service weapon at home. She hated that she'd sent Jordan away.

In the closet. Elaina's room.

Are they inside yet?

Almost.

Suddenly something crashed to the floor. It had to be the table she'd put in place. It was followed by more swearing and some stomping.

They'd given up even pretending to be subtle or quiet, either because they didn't fear the ship's security or because they didn't believe security would come.

Stay put.

She flipped her phone over, pressing the screen against Elaina's back to keep the light from reaching into the room beyond, revealing their location. But the men weren't in the bedroom yet. Their footfalls circled the living room as she pulled Elaina closer, tucking baby-soft hair under her chin. She pulled the phone away from Elaina's back to pass along one more message.

They're here.

Tell me everything you know.

A weight settled on her chest, and she had to fight for her breath. She knew what that meant. Jordan wasn't going to arrive in time. And he needed every bit of information she could give him.

Lifting Elaina into the farthest recesses of the closet, Amy whispered, "Stay put and stay silent. No matter what."

Elaina nodded, and Amy settled a plush terry-cloth robe over the girl with a quick prayer. "Lord, protect my sweet girl."

"Aunt Amy, too."

The hushed prayer made her eyes burn, and she looked heavenward with only one prayer on her heart. *God, save us. Please. Please. Please.*

And then she made her thumbs move as fast as they could across her phone, forgetting punctuation and spelling.

Two men at least
Wearing blck
Thick accent probably MidEast
Dark hair

Suddenly the bedroom door slammed open, and a dark form yanked the blankets off the bed, growling when he found it empty. "Where is she?" he yelled to his friend in the other room.

Not afraid loud

The man's form turned around the room then marched toward the bathroom. It was empty.

Next he'd check the closet. She knew that without a doubt.

Amy had only one option. Abandon her spot and try to distract them to keep them from finding Elaina.

Leaving her phone at her feet, Amy stood slowly, taking several deep breaths through her nose and releasing them slowly, silently.

The rings on the shower curtain hissed as they were wrenched across the metal bar.

It was now or never. Her only chance.

But no matter how much training and experience she'd acquired over the years, her hand shook as she twisted the handle and pushed the door open. Stepping out of the closet, she closed the door silently behind her, pressing her back against the smooth wallpaper.

The heavy step beside her interrupted her prayer.

Time to go.

She launched herself at the man, hitting him well below his center of gravity and knocking him back against the wall. His head cracked against the door frame, and he screamed.

But it didn't stop his meaty paw from slamming into the side of her face, setting off fireworks in her line of sight.

Suddenly there were two of him in front of her, and she swung at one, only to realize he was the result of double vision.

Then her arm was snapped behind her back, her shoulder blade wrenched as the man's companion joined the fray, wrapping an arm around her throat and tightening it. She sucked at the air, clawing against him, but even when her nails dug into his flesh, he didn't let up.

A kick to his companion as he pulled himself up from the floor didn't help. It only earned her another fist to the head.

The room spun and her already limited vision blurred even more.

No. No. This wasn't…

God, save Elaina.

Right before the entire world went black, she heard the wild cry of her niece.

FIVE

Jordan had never run so fast in his life. The muscles in his legs cried out for a break like they hadn't since his last week of BUD/S. And the wooden deck might as well have been beach sand for all the progress he was making.

He just couldn't move fast enough. He couldn't get from his sister's room to Michael's suite in time.

Risking a glance at his phone, he checked for another text from Amy.

She'd sent a string of texts, giving information on the men that had been only a few feet away from her. Armed and dangerous. And inside the suite.

And there had been nothing since then.

His mind immediately filled with images of Amy facing those thugs. She'd fight. She'd fight like a bobcat to protect Elaina. But as strong and well-trained as she was, the odds were sharply against her.

Had he given her a bad direction? Would she have had a better chance catching them off guard by attacking from the start? Or should he have sent her to hide elsewhere—would there have been better weapons available in the kitchen?

His heart skipped a beat.

He jumped out of the way of a couple meandering along the deck and hurdled a deck chair that had been left in the open lane.

God, let me get there.

Why had he agreed to check on Neesha and Rodney on the very opposite side of the ship? They were fine. Oblivious—which was just what he wanted for them.

So he'd taken himself out of the fight. For nothing.

Don't think about it. Don't dwell on it.

He had to keep reminding himself of that or he'd go crazy. He'd learned early in his training that if he got too far inside his own head, his body would falter. And right now, Amy and Elaina were counting on him to stay strong.

Snatching one more breath of sea air, he spun into a stairwell and bolted up the steps.

Around every corner and at every crossing, he expected to see Amy and Elaina. Perhaps it was only wishful thinking.

But surely they were being toted away from the scene.

And if they were, he was ready to fight for their freedom. His muscles tensed, and he made a stiff fist as his arms pumped to keep him moving. He was ready.

Unless she'd been…

Could she have been killed? Dean had been willing enough to shoot at her earlier. And while the men had mentioned capturing Elaina, that didn't mean they would leave her aunt alive.

Bile rose in the back of his throat as he raced down the hallway, mere steps from the ambassador's new suite. The one the captain had promised was secure. He was thirty yards away. Twenty. Ten.

So close. But everything was silent, save the droning of the ship.

There wasn't a nosy neighbor poking his head out of his cabin. No steward cleaning up. No security patrolling. And there certainly wasn't a peep coming from inside the suite. Which meant that Amy was gone…or dead.

If she'd been able to contact him, she would have.

His stomach heaved again as he crashed through the doorway, past the cracked frame and into the ransacked living room. He nearly tripped over a destroyed coffee table, two of its legs ripped clean off.

And then he realized what he was seeing. The table had been wedged against the door to keep the intruders out for as long as possible. She'd done just what he would have.

Good girl, Amy.

He took careful, silent steps around the carnage on the carpet toward Elaina's room. It, too, was silent. Only the signs of a struggle had been left behind. The ripped shower curtain in the bathroom. The overturned lamp. Amy's phone smashed as if it had been stepped on.

He knelt to pick up the pieces at the door of the closet, giving it one more cursory glance before letting out a loud sigh through tight lips.

"Elaina!"

Jordan jumped up and raced toward the cry, knowing what he'd find.

Michael Torres's eyes were wild as he surveyed the wrecked room from the doorway. When Jordan caught the ambassador's gaze, Michael flinched. "Where is my daughter? I... I didn't mean to be gone so long."

The pleading in his voice was too much, and Jordan could only shake his head.

"And Amy? Where's she?"

Jordan took a quick breath and blinked

against a strange burning at the back of his eyes. "She's gone, too."

Amy woke, clawing at her neck, but the arm that had been there was gone. And her breathing, while rapid, wasn't painful, though a swallow nearly set her throat on fire.

She blinked against the light from above in an attempt to calm the throbbing behind her eyes and rose onto her knees. Grabbing at the lip of the metal panel on the wall, she pulled herself to her feet, swaying with the motion of the room. But whether the ship was truly rolling or it was all in her head, she couldn't tell.

Squeezing her eyes closed, she leaned into the unmoving wall.

And then it all slammed back into her. The attack. The men. Elaina's screams.

"Elaina!" Her cry was hoarse as she launched herself at the metal door. It didn't budge, even when her shoulder slammed into it. She crumpled to her knees again, hanging on to the handle that refused to turn.

Elaina. She had to find her niece. Now.

There was no telling how long Amy had been out or when they'd been separated. She didn't even know where she was.

With her eyesight still slightly blurry, she took quick inventory of the room where she'd been left. It was actually more storage closet than room. Two of its walls were lined with metal shelves at least six feet high. Big plastic jugs of pink and blue cleaners filled every inch of wall space, leaving about four square feet for her to maneuver. Just enough to spin around and find exactly nothing helpful. There were no tools, no exits and no phone on the wall.

Nothing.

She heaved a sigh and turned one more time, just for good measure.

The room smelled of disinfectant and seawater, and she immediately tried to figure out where she could be in the ship that would make the saltwater smell strong enough to push the odor of cleaning products to the background. But she couldn't picture it.

Suddenly someone on the far side of the door bumped against it.

Scrambling for a place to hide, she pressed herself into the corner closest to the door, nearly tripping on a metal doorstop. The door swung out to open, but at least she could be in the last corner they'd see.

And then what?

She needed a plan, but her mind was still cloudy, still rolling with every wave. And the throbbing on the left side of her face was an ever-present reminder of the fist that had hit its mark at least twice. All the same, she concentrated on holding herself together, dealing with the moment.

Maybe there's only one.

Watch the door.

When he opens it, slam it into his head.

Great idea. *If* she knew for sure there was only one or had any clue what was waiting for her on the other side.

Before she could take another breath, she had her answer.

"What are you doing?"

The words were said by a nasally voice with a heavy accent.

"Checking on her."

And he had an American buddy, which meant there were at least two out there.

She gasped for a breath and held it, waiting for the door to open, trying to prepare her trembling muscles to fight back. But her arms felt heavier than an anchor, and when she brought her knee up in a practice kick, she barely managed to lift it to her waist. Everything inside her felt limp and weakened.

"The boss wants to see you," the first man said.

His friend grunted. "It can wait."

"They're on their way. He wants to make sure we're ready."

"We're ready," the American grumbled, but his retreating footsteps said that he'd agreed to follow his friend.

Which gave her exactly she-had-no-idea-how-long to find a way out.

She sank back against the wall, tipping her head up and whispering a quick prayer. "Lord, what am I supposed to do? I'm stuck. I'm sca-ared." She hated the way her voice caught on the word. Hated more how her chest tightened on the truth. "I'm…I need your help. I don't know…"

Her voice disappeared on a wheeze as her gaze landed on a square vent about two feet off the floor, its metal slats thin and dark. The shelves on either side of it had blocked her view before now, but it was there nonetheless. The whole cover was maybe a foot and a half wide, but she twisted her shoulders, already imagining wiggling her way into the ductwork beyond. It didn't matter where it led as long as it was far away from this cramped closet and the men who had put her here.

Pressing her ear to the door, she listened for any sign of their return. But all was silent except for a low clanging of metal against metal.

This was her chance. Maybe her only shot.

And she wasn't about to throw it away.

Diving for the grate, she jammed her fingers

into the slim margin between the metal and the wall to try to pry the cover away, but the space was too narrow. Her fingernails barely fit into the gap, and they weren't strong enough to pry the metal free.

Running her fingers around the edges, she double-checked that she hadn't missed a screw holding it in place. But she didn't find even one.

She just needed something strong and slender to wedge the grate out.

She surveyed her options. The bottles of cleaning products were useless. She needed a screwdriver or a file or some pliers.

But her captors hadn't bothered to leave her a tool set.

Letting out an impatient breath through tight lips, she closed her eyes and tried to picture everything in the room. The only empty wall was the one beside the door. Where she'd stepped on the doorstop.

Perfect.

She lunged for it, swiping it from the floor and racing the two steps back across the closet. She prayed the narrow end of the wedge was sharp enough to work as she jammed it against the metal. *Please. Please. Please.*

Only the tip slipped into the crevice, and she wanted to throw it against the wall.

"Why won't you work?"

She slammed her fist down against the door-stop. It groaned further into place.

"Yes," she whispered, giving it another hit with the heel of her hand, which ached at the treatment. Then she grabbed one of the jugs of cleaning fluid and banged it against the door-stop, forcing it to make more space between the wall and the metal. And again. And again. With each strike the doorstop sank a millimeter. Just a few more and she could leverage it to open the grate.

Suddenly the voices outside the door were back.

"Why even bother to open the door? She's still locked in there." The one with the Middle Eastern accent was still arguing against checking on her.

"I told you. We need to keep an eye on her and make sure she can't get away. She can recognize me."

His words didn't make any sense. Or maybe she was mishearing them beneath the wild tattoo of her heart to the rhythm of her internal mantra. *Quiet. Hurry. Quiet. Hurry.*

Any noise that made it through the door could give them real reason to check on her. But staying put and giving up on the grate wasn't an option.

"What do you really want to do in there?"

Oh, God.

It was the only prayer she could manage as her stomach lurched. If this man really felt threatened by her, and the idea that she might be able to identify him, then maybe he was looking for an excuse to come in and kill her.

She had to get out now.

With one final blow of the jug, the doorstop dropped into place. Grabbing the end of it, she pulled as hard as she could, jarring the metal vent cover away from the wall. It only opened up half an inch of room, but it was enough to squeeze her fingers into the crevice and pull as hard as she could.

The man with the American accent seemed to have heard the noise because he said, "I told you." Then the door handle shook.

Her heart leaped to her throat, its thundering beats surely audible even on the far side of the door.

But the door didn't open.

"Let me in," he said to his friend, who apparently had the key.

Please don't. Please, no. Hold on.

As the men continued to argue, Amy gripped the cover and pulled with everything inside her. Her arms strained and fingers burned as they slipped. *God, help me. Please.*

With one final wrench, the vent cover gave

way with a flurry of dust. Slamming one hand over her mouth to keep from coughing, she gently laid the grate on the floor with her other hand.

Bending, she stuck her head into the open shaft. The ventilation system wasn't remarkable, only a tunnel framed in metal. But eventually it would open somewhere else. By definition, it had to.

And anywhere would be better than here.

Pulling back, she glanced down at her gear. She was still in the navy-blue sundress she'd danced in at Neesha's party. Although she wasn't quite sure how much time had passed since they'd enjoyed such a carefree moment, the fabric looked like she'd slept in it for a week. It was wrinkled and crumpled and the hem had been torn. And somewhere along the way she'd lost a shoe. It wasn't the ideal outfit for this type of escape, but she'd make it work.

It wouldn't have mattered if she had been in a mascot costume. She was getting into that vent and out of Dodge.

Suddenly the argument on the other side of the door ended with a resigned, "Fine."

It was followed immediately by the sound of a key sliding into the lock.

No time to lose. She dove into the metal tunnel, pushing herself forward and wiggling against the cold flooring. The metal bowed and groaned a bit, but she didn't stop, reaching forward and clawing her way deeper into the dimness. Her body blocked some of the light from the room behind her and there wasn't much ahead.

She couldn't tell where the vent was headed, whether it dropped off or took a sharp turn.

It didn't matter.

She scrabbled her way deeper inside, pushing with her feet and squirming. Just as her feet cleared the edge of the vent, the door behind her crashed open, slamming into the wall behind it.

"What the…" The man's voice faded away before returning with a full-blast string of curses. "Where is she?"

Amy couldn't gain much traction against the slippery metal without causing a ruckus, so her movements were slow—always, always with an ear to the men in the room. When they saw the open vent, they'd know where she was.

And she prayed they'd be too big to follow her.

Also that they wouldn't have a clue where to find the exit to the vent shaft.

"She was in here. I'm telling you, I put her here myself."

The sickening thud of fist to flesh reached her, and she cringed.

"Well, then, where is she now?"

"I don't kn—" Even with his thick accent, it was clear the instant he realized the truth. "There."

Amy gave up stealth for swiftness, scrambling as fast as she could.

Hurry. Hurry. Hurry.

The staccato tattoo of her heart seemed to beat in time with the words.

Suddenly a hand latched on to the ankle of her bare foot and jerked her backward, forcing her to give up all the ground she'd gained.

"Get back here." His growl was low and lethal, and nothing could have convinced her to stay where she was.

With her remaining high heel, she gave a sharp kick in the direction she hoped was his head. His piercing scream proved that she'd hit her target as he released her.

Feet still kicking, she crawled like she had through the obstacle course all those years ago, like there was a Marine drill sergeant screaming her name and her entire future rode on it. She'd done it then so that now—with her life really on the line—she'd know she had the ability to dig deep to find whatever she needed to escape.

Her captor's string of curses died off as she reached the point where the metal made a sharp ninety degree turn to the left, putting her out of his reach. Thankfully, she'd been right in her guess that neither of the two men could fit into the vent.

"Find her. Get her back. She can't escape!"

Fingers hooked around the corner, Amy pulled herself to the end, thudding against the metal wall, and scrambled down another dim corridor.

The voices of the men faded behind her, clearly angry that they couldn't follow.

Wherever she was going, she had to get there fast.

Elaina was still out there. Somewhere.

And that man—the one who thought she could recognize him—wasn't going to stop until he made sure she'd never recognize anyone again.

SIX

The ventilation shaft took a steep dive, and Amy could do nothing to keep from picking up speed as she slid down. Curling her shoulder against her ear, she braced for impact a moment before she crashed into the wall at the bottom of the chute.

Readjusting her position, she flexed her right hand to ward off any numbness from the harsh impact and took in her surroundings. The wall she'd slid into was the top of a T, each side reaching out until it was lost to darkness. But to her left, the darkness was interrupted by small pockets of light, representing glimmers of hope.

She scrambled in that direction, slipping against the cold metal. After several long minutes, she reached an illuminated patch and discovered the source of the light. A wall vent was tucked into a small alcove, and there was just enough room to lie on her back and wedge her feet against the slats of the vent's cover. With a careful kick, she sent the grate crashing into the room.

A woman shrieked, but Amy wasn't deterred. She slipped through the opening feetfirst and dropped to the floor of a small cabin.

The majority of the room was taken up with a queen-size bed; a pile of towels sat in the center of the duvet. A woman in a gray uniform cowered on the far side of the room, her hands covering her mouth and eyes wide.

"I'm sorry," Amy said. The words were scratchy at best, so she reached out her hand as though she could calm the maid's fears. "It's okay. I'm just…"

There wasn't any *just* about it. And there certainly wasn't an easy way to explain why she'd popped out of a wall. So she pointed at the door. "I'll go." But then she looked down at the grate still on the floor and scooped it up to shove it back into place.

"I think I should call my supervisor." The maid pushed herself out of the corner and squared her shoulders. Her voice was shaky, but she seemed determined.

Amy glanced over her shoulder and stared hard at the young woman. "Yes. You probably should." She wrinkled her forehead, playing out possible scenarios for a split second before adding, "But don't expect me to wait around to meet her. I'll be talking to the captain soon enough."

The maid only blinked in response as Amy made a dash for the door. But before she shut it behind her, she turned back for a little clarification. "Can you tell me where we are?"

"The bottom deck."

Basically steerage. Perfect. She glanced down at the gray dust that now covered her skin and most of her dress and tried not to think about how many people she'd run into between here and...

Well, here and finding help. And then finding Elaina.

She set off down the hallway, but in only a few steps she grew annoyed with the uneven gait from wearing one shoe. After ripping off her heel, she held it and ran.

The hallway wasn't crowded, but neither was it empty. Many people stared at her as she raced along the carpet. A mom pulled her children out of the way, and Amy tried to smile in response.

But she couldn't make herself feel anything but urgency. The pounding of her feet echoed a terrible cadence playing in her head. *Get there. Get there.*

But where was *there*? Where was her precious niece being held?

When she reached the elevator bank, she

paused for breath and tried to wrap her mind around where she needed to go.

She had no idea where Elaina had been taken. She didn't even know where *she'd* been kept.

Glancing back down the hallway, she quickly mapped out where she'd ended up. And if she'd gone down at least one—but maybe two—decks within the air shaft, she couldn't have been held anywhere on the lowest level. She'd gone left and left again to end up on the starboard side of the ship.

The elevator dinged, and she paused her mental mapping.

Maybe she could find her way back to the storage room. Maybe not. But she couldn't risk it alone. Not when there were definitely men looking for her. She had to talk to the captain. And then she had to find backup.

And there was only one man on this ship she trusted to watch her six.

Jordan was ready to punch a hole through the wall.

So far, he'd been able to find no sign of Amy or Elaina. It was like they'd vanished. In the middle of the sea.

He jogged back toward the ambassador's second suite—the one where the abduction had taken place—hoping the security guards who had arrived after Torres was whisked away to his third cabin had found something Jordan had overlooked in the room.

Unlikely.

But he'd never wanted to be wrong more in his life.

As he rounded a corner into the final stretch of hallway, a bit of navy blue fabric fluttered and then disappeared. An image of Amy in her blue sundress—that same color—flashed across his mind's eye. Then it was gone.

Whoever was wearing that shade of blue seemed to have gone into Torres's suite, but there were too many doors—and a handful of guests coming and going—between his position and his destination to be entirely sure.

Perhaps his eyes were playing tricks on him.

No. That couldn't be.

He trusted his vision. He had to. His entire career was based on being certain that what he saw through his scope was true. His eyes didn't play tricks on him.

And if his memory wasn't faulty either, then Amy could be back.

His heart skipped a beat, and his feet kicked into a higher gear.

After weaving through pockets of other passengers, he finally arrived at the damaged door and stopped in his tracks.

There she was. Her long, slender arms were crossed at the wrist over her chest—one hand, strangely, held her shoe—as she made a slow circle, surveying the destruction for the first time in the light of day. Her bare feet turned in quarter steps. Everything about her, except for her eyes, seemed cloudy, subdued. Her bronze skin was almost gray.

He'd never seen anything quite so wonderful.

She looked up in his direction just as she completed her turn. Her eyes flashed open even wider. And somehow he was across the room and pulling her into a hug before he even realized he was moving.

"Amy." It came out as barely a breath as he pressed his cheek to the top of her head.

Her arms wound around his waist, holding him tight, as she pressed her face into his chest. "I'm okay. I'm fine." Suddenly she tried to pull away, but he couldn't let her go just yet. "I'm gross."

She wiggled free, but not all the way. He kept his hands on her arms, holding her near, sweeping his gaze over her to confirm she was there. Safe.

"I'm so gross," she repeated. "I'm covered in dirt."

"Do I look like I care?"

Her forehead wrinkled and then released with her sweet laugh.

But her humor wasn't enough to erase the memories of the night before. "I thought you were gone." His heart picked up and his voice nearly failed him as he relived the moment when he'd seen her smashed phone and thought for a brief moment he'd never see her alive again. "You *were* gone."

"I was." Her lip trembled for just a moment, but she bit into it hard as her eyes seemed to look right through him. "I knew there were two of them, and that I wouldn't be able to take them both down, but we couldn't hide forever. When he came into the room—" she swung her head toward Elaina's door and winced at the action "—I couldn't wait. Inside the closet, we were trapped. I ducked out when he checked the bathroom, and when he came back out I went for his knees."

Her muscles tensed beneath his grip, clearly recalling the rush of adrenaline it had taken to attack a man probably twice her size. And Jordan could do nothing but listen as he ran his hands down to her elbows and back up to her shoulders, squeezing gently, praying firmly.

God, let me catch whoever is responsible for this.

Her fingers touched her throat, drawing attention to the purple mark there. "The other man got his arm around me here." There wasn't even a tremor in her voice, and he wanted to tell her that he knew lifelong sailors with less gumption. But she seemed to need to say this, and he couldn't risk having her shut down.

"He clocked me hard on my cheek." Her hand moved to the bruise there. "I thought that was it. When I felt myself start to pass out, I figured they'd get rid of me on the spot."

He'd thought the same thing. But it wouldn't do either of them a bit of good to say as much, so he clamped his lips closed and nodded, prodding her on.

She didn't take the hint. Instead the distance in her gaze deepened.

"What happened after that?"

She shook her head slowly and pinched her eyes closed. "I heard Elaina scream. I heard her, but I couldn't fight back. I couldn't get to her."

"Did you see her again after you blacked out?"

"No." She opened her eyes slowly. "I woke up in a storage closet. It was locked, and I heard at least two guards on the other side of the door."

Something like hope sprouted inside him. If he could get to where she had been held, maybe there'd be someone still lurking around or a clue to help their search. "Where is it?"

Amy's eyes flashed with something close to regret. "I'm not sure."

How could she not be sure? Hadn't she paid attention to her surroundings when she'd escaped? *Keep track of where you've been and where you're going.* That was basic military training. And Marines were better than basic. She hadn't been with the DEA so long that she'd forgotten. "Why?"

"I escaped through an air vent, and I didn't have a ready map."

There was a touch of sarcasm in her last words, and despite everything else going on, he had to smile. "Well, if that's the excuse you want to go with."

Squaring her shoulders, she stared him down as though she could read his doubts. "I *was* paying attention, but it's not easy to count off strides when you're crawling through metal tubing in a dress with one shoe." She held up her blue strappy sandal, and he was suddenly glad she hadn't thrown it at him. He probably deserved it.

"I'm pretty sure it was on either the second or third level from the bottom. I slid down a good section and ended up in a cabin on the lowest deck."

That made sense. "What's on those levels?"

"I don't know, but I thought the captain might

be able to help. There have to be blueprints for the ship, right?"

"Sure."

She looked around quickly, like she was just now realizing where she was. "I thought Michael would be here."

"The captain set him up in a new cabin, and security was supposed to be searching this room for clues."

"Oh. Right. I...I should have realized that." Her mouth dropped open, her eyes blinking slowly for several silent seconds. He had a sudden urge to pull her into his arms again. To hold her until his heart returned to a normal speed. To reassure her that it would be all right.

But all the reassurances in the world couldn't make her safe, or return her niece to her side. A promise didn't guarantee an outcome. After all, his dad had promised that he'd be back at the end of his shift. He'd promised to be at Jordan's Little League game. He'd promised to take the family to the movies that weekend.

He'd made a lot of promises he hadn't been able to keep.

Jordan refused to do the same.

Some things couldn't be controlled, but some could. And not making promises about the uncontrollable was one he could do. It hurt too badly to be the one left with broken promises.

Amy licked her lips in a slow, thoughtful motion, and suddenly her fear fell away. She shrugged and straightened. "We need to talk to the captain. He has to know what's going on on his ship. And we need to find Michael. I want to know who called him last night, and why he was away from the room for so long. It seems like too much of a coincidence for the attackers to come when he and Pete weren't there. And I want to know everything he's mixed up in. Something isn't adding up. We have to figure out what trouble Michael's in."

"Yes, ma'am." He gave her a mock salute, and she cracked a half smile before shaking her head. Yes, he was teasing her—but he agreed with her, too. He'd been thinking the same thing. Michael had to be their next step.

"And Neesha?"

Her words hit a gut punch. "You think she's part of this?"

Eyes wide with surprise, Amy shook her head. "No. Of course not. I just want to make sure she's safe. Did you tell her what's going on?"

He laughed, breathy and bitter. "I'm not even sure *I* know what's going on." But Amy's gaze didn't shift, and the intensity there held him in place. "She was fine when I saw her last night. But I haven't told her about Elaina—or that you'd been take-en." He swallowed the catch in his throat—the one that said if he never spent another night sweating her absence, it would be too soon—and tried to force a smile into place.

Amy's eyes narrowed for a split second, and he felt like a bug under a microscope, unable to hide from her inspection. And then she gave a small shake of her head and stepped back.

"Sure. No reason to scare Neesha. This is still her wedding trip," she said. He nodded in agreement. "And we're going to get Elaina back before Neesha has to know anything."

"But first, maybe we should find you some shoes."

She glanced down, and her grin flashed for a brief moment. "That would be nice. And maybe a shower and some clean clothes."

"And some water and a bite to eat." He flipped the tip of one of her curls, which was surprisingly soft. "And even a brush for your hair."

She swatted at his hand and moved toward the door. "I just need to be in something easier to run in. Easier to fight in."

"You think they're going to be coming after you again?"

"I know it."

She sounded dead serious and absolutely certain in a way that struck him hard in the chest, and he rubbed at a spot in the center as though he could soothe the strange ache. "What makes you so sure? They're after Elaina, right? They have her, so why waste time looking for you?"

She stopped abruptly and he nearly ran into her back. "I didn't tell you." It wasn't really a question, but there was a hint of surprise in her voice. "I wasn't thinking... The men guarding the storage closet. I heard them when I was escaping."

He narrowed his gaze and leaned in close like that might help him hear her better. "What did they say?"

"One of them—he had a nondescript American accent—wanted to get rid of me. He said that I might recognize him."

Jordan released a quick breath, wishing the tension at that spot in his chest would let go as easily. "Did you see him? See his face or any distinguishing markers?"

She shook her head hard and fast. "No." Then she chewed on her lower lip for a long second. "It was so strange. Of course I didn't see him. At least not clearly. It was dark, and his face was in the shadow, and I went for his knees. I only really saw his legs. He hit me in the head, so by the time I saw his face, there were two of him. Both blurry. Then I was out cold.

"Even then, why would it matter if I could recognize him?"

His stomach took a sharp dive as he rubbed his hands together slowly. *Think, Somerton. Think.*

But there were too many questions, and intel was sparse.

He took quick inventory of what he knew. Michael had received an unexpected phone call, and kidnappers had taken advantage of that to abduct his daughter. Elaina was still missing. Someone thought Amy could recognize him. And he'd be looking to silence her.

A shiver raced down his spine, and he tried to shake it off.

It didn't work.

The tingling sensation only traveled to his arms and down to his hands, no matter how tightly he squeezed his fists. It was a reminder that he was personally involved. But how could he not be?

She was Neesha's best friend. He'd known her most of his life. And he still had to figure out a way to apologize for the debacle at his aunt's house last winter when he'd so thoroughly embarrassed her.

Their lives were entwined. Amy was in danger. A child he knew was missing. Of course he had a personal connection.

That shiver didn't mean anything more.

He wouldn't let it.

Shoving aside his wayward train of thought, he circled back to the last place he'd been. Intel. He had to get some more information, and he had to keep Amy safe.

"Just let me get cleaned up," Amy said. "I'll be five minutes, tops." She made her way toward the door, but he stopped her with a gentle hand around her arm.

"Maybe you should stay with Neesha and Rodney."

Her eyes lit with fire as if he'd just insulted her momma. "You did not just say that to me."

"Listen, Amy." He let go of her arm and scrubbed at the dome of his head. "Someone's looking for you, and we don't even know who he is."

Her narrowing eyes had him second-guessing his tactic, but he'd started down this path. It was probably too late to back out now. "I'm only saying that these guys are armed. We're not. It could be dangerous." Man, he sounded stupid.

He was stupid.

And she didn't have to say a word for him to know she agreed with that assessment wholeheartedly. The pinch of her lips and lines between her perfectly arched eyebrows told him everything he needed to know.

Finally she took a little breath. "I believe what you meant to say was that you've been sniper backup for Marines before, and you'd be honored to do so again."

A bubble of laughter caught in his throat. The situation was the furthest thing from funny, but Amy was amazing and in the running to be his favorite partner. His swim buddy and best friend since SEAL training, Zach McCloud, was great, but Zach rarely jabbed at Jordan the way Amy just had. And he didn't even know he'd been missing out on it.

Amy was his favorite combination of whip-smart woman and stunning field agent. Regardless of the nine inches and seventy-five pounds he had on her, she wasn't going to back down.

Coughing back the chuckle, he nodded slowly. "Absolutely. That's exactly what I meant. I'm glad we're on the same page."

"Good." With a curt nod she marched out of the room, her back ramrod straight. Whatever light Michael would shed on this situation and whatever they faced, she'd go after it the same way, chin high and eyes focused.

They were both going to need that same determination to get Elaina back.

SEVEN

Amy was a breath away from strangling her brother-in-law. She sucked in air deeply through her nose and released it slowly through tight lips, but the breathing exercise wasn't helping to calm her down. After fifteen minutes of questioning, he was still far too hesitant to share any information about the political issues that might have led to the kidnapping of his daughter.

"Michael, you have to tell us. You understand that Elaina's life is on the line, right?"

The ambassador paused in his slow pacing of the room and shook his head. "I know. But I don't have any information. Nothing that will help."

From his place propped against the wall next to the cabin door, Jordan caught her eye. His big body looked relaxed, but there was a fire in his eyes that promised her she wasn't alone in believing that Michael was lying to them.

"Isn't it possible that someone called you so

that you and Pete would leave your room so they could come for Elaina?" She tried to keep her voice even as she worked through the scenario in her own mind. But the pieces didn't fall into place.

"It wasn't about her. The call came from the State Department in Washington, and that's all I can tell you."

Jordan sniffed, quiet but questioning. "Do you trust the person who called you?"

Michael sank to the couch and dropped his head into his hands with a sigh. "I have no reason not to."

They were getting nowhere. And they were moving at a turtle's pace on the way.

Amy pressed a hand to her chest and tried to stop the fist that seemed to clench her lungs. When that didn't work, she stalked across the room, stopped at a porthole and stared across a mile of smooth blue. It was calm outside, but her insides held a raging storm.

It was Jordan who finally ended the silence. "What about the death threats that you mentioned before?"

She spun and stared at Jordan before letting her gaze jump to Michael, who looked just as surprised about the question. They'd covered this already.

Jordan scratched at the top of his head, right

where his hair was growing back after a close shave. He worked his jaw a few times, his eyes looking toward the ceiling. He appeared to be mentally sorting through the same mixed-up puzzles she was. But maybe he had better pieces to work with. She prayed it was true.

"This person, who called you last night—" Jordan's gaze dropped to spear Michael "—do they know about the threats?"

"What does it matter?" Michael stood again and resumed pacing the length of the couch. "Why are we still talking about the phone call? Why aren't you out there looking for her? Why am *I* not looking for her?" He marched toward the door, and his mostly useless shadow of a bodyguard followed, but Jordan held up his hand to stop them both.

"We have been. We will again." Jordan's voice was smooth as silk, but there was a steel bar running through it, calm, collected, sure. "But if we're going to be able to find her and keep her safe, we have to know what we're up against. Who these guys are and why they've taken her will help us guess how many there are, how they're armed and how willing they are to die."

Michael's swallow was audible as his Adam's apple bobbed. "Why would they want to die?"

Jordan's eyebrows rose, his forehead wrinkled in waves for a split second. "Are you playing naive, Mr. Ambassador? You've spent the better part of three years in a country more or less run by terrorists. You know that terrorist leaders are able to cultivate a loyalty that will lead others to commit terrible crimes and willingly lay down their own lives in the process."

"But—but those are terrorists."

Jordan pointed his finger into the hallway and nodded. "They sure aren't candy stripers. And whoever they're working for has them convinced that human life is disposable."

Michael looked visibly stunned, like he hadn't quite realized the extent of the situation, and it made Amy sick. How could he be so smart, such a savvy politician and also so extremely myopic? It wasn't like him. It wasn't normal. And it was keeping them from getting the information they needed to rescue Elaina, which infuriated her.

She stormed past him, banging her shoulder into his just for the flash of pain in the process.

Michael jerked back, slapping a hand to the point where they'd connected, and she looked back to see tears welling in his eyes. Suddenly he fell to the couch, covered his face with his hands and let out a terrible sob. "They're going to kill her!"

"Who?" Jordan left the wall and nearly hurdled the couch to drop by Michael's side.

Amy couldn't seem to get her muscles to move. She stared in silence as Jordan asked the pointed question.

"Who's going to kill her?"

"I don't know. They didn't identify themselves. They were on the phone when I got to the captain's office, and they told me not to contact the authorities or call for help. Or even tell a security guard. I'm not supposed to tell anyone—especially not you." Once the floodgates opened, he seemed unable to stop, the words tumbling out without thought or order. "He said they have eyes on me, and if I did anything like that, they're going to kill Elaina. I'll never see her again."

The panic in his voice couldn't be faked, and it tore through her even harder than her own fear.

"Did they tell you what they want?"

"No. But they said they're watching me, and they have big plans for me."

"Big plans?" Amy dropped to the opposite couch and leaned forward, trying to read anything on Michael's face through his fingers.

He looked up from his hands and nodded slowly. "That's exactly what they said. I don't know what they want from me. I tried to get them to give up Elaina and take me instead, but they just laughed."

Jordan rubbed his hands together, his forearms still resting on his knees. "They must have something on the burner. After all, they're expecting someone else to arrive."

Michael jumped, jerking his gaze to Jordan. "Do you have any idea what it is they're after?"

"I don't. But they don't want you. They want to control you. And Elaina's the best way to do that. They know you'd do anything to keep her safe. And they're going to ask for the moon."

"I can't give them the moon. I can't give them anything." Michael's voice had taken on a panicked tone, and Amy reached for his arm to give it a gentle squeeze.

"It's going to be okay."

Jordan stood and laid a big hand on Michael's shoulder. "We'll find Elaina. You don't have to fear them."

Michael jumped to his feet, too. "I'm going with you."

"No, you're not. You're going to stay here with Pete. You're not going to let anyone into this room, and you're going to let those eyes on you think that you're complying."

Michael looked at Amy and suddenly reached out to hug her. "Be safe. Find my girl."

"We will." She marched past Jordan and out the door, letting it slam behind her.

In the next instant it opened again, and Jordan followed her with one final warning to Michael. "And don't talk to Neesha. If I find out you ruined her wedding..."

The warning died off as the door slapped closed again.

And then it was just the two of them in the hallway—well, them and a raucous family leaving their suite a few doors down. Amy ignored the others and stared hard into Jordan's deep brown eyes, trying and failing to read what he was thinking.

"What's wrong with him?" she finally whispered. "Why didn't he just tell us?"

He reached for her hands, his calloused fingers wrapping around hers. "He's afraid. Maybe it was the best he could do."

She ripped her hands free of his grasp and slammed them on her hips. "That's worse."

And it was. She and Alexandra had heard that over and over growing up. *He's doing the best he can*, their mom had said.

Well, his best wasn't good enough. Not her father's. And certainly not Michael's.

And neither was Jordan's. Not when he'd embarrassed her and then—on the date that he'd planned, as a way to make it up to her for the previous debacle—he'd left her waiting, her hair done and in a new dress that had cost more than a month's worth of groceries. He'd left her waiting for what felt like hours, every minute just like her childhood. Waiting. Waiting. Forgotten.

Jordan had convinced her once that she could trust him with more than a mission. And it was almost like he was trying to again.

She wouldn't be so gullible this time.

Instead she took a deep breath. "I'm going to find her."

"I'm going with you."

She shook her head, her heart battling with her head. She could use his help, but every minute with him was another reminder that she'd sat on her couch waiting for too long. "You don't have to."

His laugh was completely devoid of humor. "You're kidding, right? I know I'm not a blood relation, but I still care about her." And there was something else he didn't say, something that lingered in the air for a long moment and almost seemed to imply that Elaina wasn't the only member of her family that he cared about. But Amy didn't ask for clarification. She didn't want it. She just wanted to get moving, to do something.

"Maybe it would be better if we split up." She'd meant it entirely in relation to finding her niece, but for a moment he looked like she'd slapped him in the face, like she'd ended a relationship they'd never had.

He recovered quickly, and a sarcastic grin settled over his lips. "I thought you said you needed sniper backup."

"I never said I needed it." Wow, she sounded hostile. But how was she supposed to tone it down now when everything he did made her want to simultaneously throw her shoe—the high-heeled one—at him and fall back into his arms. Not that she'd liked his comfort.

She had not.

At all.

Except maybe a little tiny bit.

And later she would find that bit and extinguish it.

If he had been anyone else in the world, she would have expected him to put his hands up and surrender. He wasn't. He didn't. Instead he put his hands behind his back and leaned forward, towering over her just enough to make her blood boil. Again.

"Agent Delgado, I'll be your backup or your sidekick or anything else you want to call me. But I'm not letting you out of my sight again."

His eyes flashed, and her stomach swirled, and she wanted to scream—but she refused to show him that he affected her that strongly.

"As far as I can tell, we have two options." He ticked off one finger. "We can either attempt to find the closet where you were being held and pray that Elaina is somewhere nearby." Then he ticked off another. "Or we can see if a night in the holding cell has made our friend Eric Dean more talkative. I was thinking… Well, where would you suggest we start?"

"I suggest you quit pretending you don't have an opinion."

That made him laugh, rich and real and contagious. She couldn't help her own spurt of a giggle that followed. The tension that had made her neck stiff and shoulders sore was still there. But, somehow, by his side, it was a little easier to carry.

"I think we should start with Eric. I'd still rather know what we're looking for than what we're not."

"But Elaina—"

"Is still on the ship. They'd have to bring a helicopter or a boat in to get her out of here. And as far as we know, no one else has *arrived*." He leaned heavily on the last word, a reminder that the man who chased her had had information about the someone else who was going to join them.

Suddenly the disorientation she'd felt when she woke up alone in that closet returned, making her head spin and her breath catch. And Elaina had, or was going to have, that same experience. Or worse.

She grabbed his forearm and dug her fingers into his flesh. "We have to get to her."

To his credit, he never flinched as he gently removed her grip, one finger at a time. "Let's figure out where she is first. And then I promise—I'll do everything in my power to help her."

It wasn't quite the promise she wanted. It wasn't a guarantee of Elaina's safe return.

But maybe it was enough for now.

There was an inherent problem with the idea that someone was chasing Amy because he thought she could identify him when she really couldn't. It meant that someone was watching for them, knowing exactly what they looked like, while they could walk right past Amy's attacker and not realize it was him until it was too late.

It left Jordan to trail her across the ship and pray that they weren't spotted. There were only so many back passageways and closed stairwells they could take on the way to the security office. And if she was spotted and targeted first, her pursuer could be on top of them without a shred of notice. Or worse, he could take a position and get off a handful of shots before Jordan even knew there was imminent danger.

Jordan closed the distance between himself and Amy, his chest nearly touching her back.

She didn't slow down, but she shot him a sharp glare over her shoulder. It clearly said he should take this opportunity to back off.

He responded with a look that he hoped said that wasn't going to happen on his watch.

She picked up her speed, and he stayed on her six, trying not to notice the way her curls bounced with each step or her subtle vanilla scent as it wafted off her.

Before they rounded the final corner to the security office, the sounds of an argument reached them. At first the words were muffled, though clearly agitated. But as they turned into the hallway, the reason for the disagreement became clear.

"Where is he?" The short man had his back to them, but Jordan knew that voice, even in a growl. Staff Captain Xavier.

The other man was dressed in a deep blue security uniform, his hands clasped behind his back and facial features tight. He shook his head frantically. "I told you. I don't know."

"That's not good enough. You've been on guard duty all night." Xavier got into the younger man's face, stretching to his full height and wagging a finger beneath his nose. "How did you not see anything? He couldn't have just escaped."

Amy pulled up short, and Jordan nearly ran into her, grabbing her arms to stop himself from sending both of them to the floor. She glanced at him, and he nodded as icy fingers slowly made their way into his chest.

Neither the guard nor the staff captain had uttered a name, but they both knew.

Eric Dean—their only source of information on the kidnappers aboard the ship—had disappeared.

The security guard hung his head low. "I must have fallen asleep, sir. But I don't understand it—I wasn't even tired. I've worked every night since we left port in Miami. I drank my coffee like always, and I was fine. But then all of a sudden I woke up, and he was gone."

"Did anyone else come into the security office?"

"Only you, sir."

Xavier stabbed his fingers through his salt-and-pepper hair and growled low in his throat, just loud enough to carry to Jordan and Amy. "That's not good enough. We have people in—" He turned a bit and must have caught sight of them because he suddenly whipped all the way around. Lips tight and brow furrowed, he nodded at them.

Amy stayed rooted to the garish blue carpet, so Jordan stepped around her, reaching out his hand toward Xavier. "Sounds like bad news."

"I'm afraid so." His handshake was limp, his gaze curious as it reached past Jordan's shoulder and focused on Amy. "I'm…I'm surprised to see you here. I had heard from the captain last night. He said there was an issue. Mr. Torres explained…"

That explained the confusion on Xavier's face. He knew that Amy had been taken, and apparently he thought she couldn't handle a reminder, so he tiptoed around the subject. He didn't know Amy. And he hadn't counted on her resourcefulness and ability to escape. That was classic underestimating. Amy was tougher than most gave her credit for.

She was tougher than Jordan had thought, too. He'd known she was stubborn, of course. No one easygoing would have hung on to a grudge for a year just because he'd canceled a date and said something stupid in front of his family.

But Amy had.

Tenacious. Stubborn. The kind of woman who would crawl a mile through a nasty, dirty air duct to free herself and find her niece.

The staff captain had no idea who he was dealing with.

Suddenly she was by his side, her shoulder nearly pressed against his.

"Dean is gone?" she asked. "But where? When?"

Xavier shot a scowl at his subordinate. "We're looking into that. But we don't have any solid leads at the moment."

"Can we look around?"

With a small shake of his head, Xavier said, "It would be best if you didn't distract the personnel in there. We're still running a full security operation."

Not very well, as far as Jordan could see.

He had to clench his fist and bite his tongue to keep from saying it out loud. Amy was the one who rescued him from offending the staff captain.

"Do you have any indication where my niece may be? Any tips from passengers about strange activity?"

"No." His word was clipped, but something about the stoop in Amy's shoulders must have prodded him to elaborate. "But that's not unusual. Passengers on a cruise are so focused on the fun and the food that they don't pay attention to what's going on around them. I'd say at least three-quarters of our current guests are from cold-weather climates. They're just so happy to be out of the snow and ice that they can't see past the swimming pool.

"And the ambassador said he didn't want to alert the other passengers. He thought it might trigger the kidnappers, who could hurt his daughter."

Amy nodded. Jordan sighed. It was a fair cover story, but Jordan knew that Michael had been thoroughly frightened by the call he'd received the night before.

"But my team and I will keep an eye out for anything unusual."

"We'd appreciate it."

Xavier reached into his shirt pocket and pulled out a white card. "Here's my direct line. You can call it from any phone on the ship. If I don't answer, someone from my team will. Now, if you'll excuse me, I need to deal with…" He tipped his head toward the security officer still behind him.

Jordan led Amy back the way they'd come and didn't stop until they'd reached a secluded spot. Then he stopped her short with a hand on her elbow and leaned low to tell her what he was thinking, but she beat him to it.

"Something is way off here."

"I know." He scrubbed the top of his head with his knuckles. "How do you just lose a detainee?"

"And why was there only one guy guarding him?" Amy added. "There should be two always. Everywhere. That's basic stuff."

He nodded. In BUD/S they were called swim buddies—the guy you knew had your back no matter what. But the navy wasn't the only branch of service that knew the importance of working in teams. From schoolchildren to fire fighters to military people, they all employed the buddy system.

So how had an experienced staff captain allowed one man to let another escape?

It was a ridiculous question. "He didn't escape on his own."

"I know. Someone let him out." Amy worked on her lower lip with her teeth and twirled one of her curls around a finger. "My guess is someone laced the guard's coffee."

He'd been thinking the same thing and picked right up with her. "A double dose of ground-up standard sleeping pills would do the trick."

"Probably."

"Which means—"

She cut him off with the exact words he'd been about to say. "Someone on the inside is helping Dean and probably a whole terrorist cell."

"You need to be careful." The words popped out before he even thought about them. They were true, but they wouldn't have been his usual warning to his partner. But they were the first thing to pop into his mind.

Her nose flared and eyebrows pinched together. "Me? Why just me? You're not bulletproof, you know."

"Why, Amy." He fluttered a hand in front of his face and batted his lashes in his best impression of a Southern belle. "With all that sweet talk, I might start to think you really care."

She rolled her eyes at him. "Seriously, Somerton? We're about to go into a thicket of terrorists, and you're making jokes?"

"If—" The words got stuck and he cleared his throat before trying again. "If I didn't laugh in the downtime, I'd never get to laugh. And that seems like a pretty sorry life."

Her lips dipped into a thoughtful frown, but the corners of her eyes wrinkled like she was fighting a smile.

And suddenly he wanted that smile. Not just because it was beautiful—which it was. He wanted her to smile because he'd caused it. He wanted to make her laugh and see the light shining in her eyes because she liked being around him.

He wanted her to like him.

Not for his sniper skills or the Trident pin that marked him as a SEAL. Not for his bank account, which was pretty anemic, anyway. And certainly not for his face, which he'd been told by more than one woman was fairly attractive.

He just wanted her to like him for him, for Jordan the man.

The realization made his head spin, but there was no turning off the truth.

They'd been at odds for so long that he'd forgotten he genuinely liked her.

It wasn't as though he'd ever go back on his promise to himself, though. So long as he had a job that put him in the line of danger, he wouldn't be in a relationship.

Not that he'd think about Amy in those terms, anyway.

But that didn't stop him from enjoying an interaction with a female friend.

He grinned hard, trying to get Amy to follow his lead. But she shook her head.

"You're ridiculous."

Was that a note of humor in her voice?

"You make it sound like a bad thing," he said.

"I do not." She didn't give him time to continue the argument, waving her hand to push the conversation behind them. "Where are we going? To find that storage room?"

"Sure. Do you have what you need?"

Her hand immediately went to her waist and

the holster that should have been there. "I guess so. You?"

He smiled, commiserating—he missed the weight of his rifle—and nodded. "Same."

They took off for a back stairwell, moving silently and in sync, Amy leading. She kept a hand pressed the wall, balancing as they moved downward, quickly but steady enough to keep from drawing attention. Voices above them echoed across the metal steps, but they didn't see anyone until they reached the second level.

Amy cracked the door open and poked her head out, immediately ducking back into relative cover.

"What's out there?"

Her lips pursed to the side. "Staff. House-keepers, cooks, busboys. All in uniform."

"Makes sense, I guess. We can't be far from the kitchen, can we?"

She nodded. "And I was put in a supply closet. Maybe near the housekeeping HQ?"

"Makes sense to me." He wiggled between her and the door and peeked into a hubbub of activity. Kitchen staff in their ivory jackets pushed carts of food toward a service elevator, jockeying for position with the housekeeping units barreling down the narrow hallway. A variety of uniforms hustled to their destinations, generally with heads bowed, focused on their tasks.

"It would be easy to be overlooked here, wouldn't it?"

"I'm sure that's why they chose this spot," he said. "They probably put you in a laundry cart, covered you with a sheet and strolled right past a hundred other people."

She shivered. "Well, let's try to blend in." Shooting him a glance that said it might be harder for him, she ducked through the door, and he had no choice but to follow.

He did stick out in the crowd—and not just because he wasn't wearing a uniform. His eyes were higher than the top of every other head in the hall. But at least that gave him a clear view of the general layout and the people packed into the buzzing throng. The air smelled of soap and bleach and a sharp fish dish that cut through everything else.

He bent to whisper in her ear. "Does anything look familiar?"

"I was unconscious. Remember?"

Right. Obviously. So what exactly were they looking for?

"The door was metal, and it had a silver-colored handle. At least, on the inside."

"Sure." He bit his tongue to keep from pointing out that all the doors were metal with silver-colored handles. It wouldn't be helpful, especially when it was pretty clear from her slowly stooping shoulders that Amy didn't have a clue where they were going.

He hadn't really expected her to.

But he'd hoped. For Elaina's sake. For Amy's sake.

He'd wanted at least a clue.

Instead they were going to end up empty-handed. Again.

As they neared the end of the hallway, metal pans thundered against each other and the din of voices picked up.

The words jumbled together to make mostly nonsense, but Amy held up her hand and stopped so suddenly that the women behind him slammed into his back. The maid immediately stepped around him, shooting him a scowl and mumbling something under her breath.

Jordan shifted Amy out of the main flow of traffic as her eyes darted in every direction.

"I remember the sound of clashing pots and pans. I could hear it in the closet. They were muffled, but I'm sure of it. I couldn't have been far away."

He looked around, following her lead, but nothing struck him as unusual or out of place. It was just the ship's bustling hub.

"Well." He shrugged, only one ridiculous plan

playing in his mind. "If you were down here, then maybe Elaina is, too."

"I hope so." Her voice barely reached him over the din, but her movements were sure. Before he could even tell her his wild idea, she'd implemented it, grabbing the nearest door handle. The door swung open, and an invisible cloud of steam swept over them. Industrial washers and dryers clanked and tumbled in the relatively shallow room.

As she stepped inside, she looked over her shoulder and silently challenged him not to follow.

They'd already decided that wasn't an option, so he ducked after her, checking every nook and cranny.

They poked into every open door and knocked on the few locked ones, but there was no sign of the storage closet. And no indication that Elaina had ever been there. Everything looked exactly as it should.

But they knew the truth.

This was only a facade covering something sinister.

And the sinister knew how to hide.

As they exited another empty laundry room, Amy sighed. "I don't understand. I thought for sure that we'd find something."

"I know." He wanted to pull her into his arms. To comfort her. As a friend would.

But somehow he knew that she wouldn't appreciate that, so he pointed upward. "Let's regroup and figure out our next steps. Maybe Xavier has some new information about—"

A sudden commotion at the entrance to the kitchen jerked his attention away from her and made his skin crawl. Every hair on his arms stood on end as voices raised.

"I'm telling you, I saw her." The voice had an American accent, and Amy's entire countenance changed when it registered with her.

She whipped around and stared toward the man, but she didn't have Jordan's height or his vantage to look over the heads of the crowd.

"There are two of them." He kept his voice low and spoke directly into her ear, even as a shiver racked her whole body. "One blond and the other definitely Middle Eastern."

"Where? Where is she?" the blond man screamed in a high-pitched voice, pushing people aside and crashing into a service cart.

With closed eyes, Amy said, "That's him."

Jordan didn't wait for her to repeat herself. He simply spread his hand across the small of her back and steered her between obstacles.

"Where did she go?" the high-pitched voice said again. "Find her!"

The clatter of a bumped cart and the hollers of an angry housekeeper behind them threatened to steal his attention, but he forced his gaze to methodically sweep the path ahead. Back and forth, checking for potential hurdles.

Amy's pace picked up with each step, and he used his free hand on her arm to keep her pace more casual. "Don't draw attention," he cautioned her. "Not until we get to the stairs."

She gave him a curt nod, and he focused on following his own instructions. It was so much easier to say than to do with a man looking for her in the bustling crowd. The same with keeping his breathing even when his lungs wanted to burst and his body ached to make a break for it.

"Get over here. Help me out!"

Jordan risked a glance over his shoulder to see three more men join the blond. All wore jackets with conspicuous bulges. Even without his training, he'd have recognized that they each carried a weapon.

His heart lodged in his throat. This was not the place to take them on. It couldn't be. So he forced a warning past the pounding at his Adam's apple. "He's got more company."

She sucked in a loud breath, and he took it as confirmation that she understood. They were outnumbered, outarmed and in the middle of a ship full of defenseless civilians.

He couldn't afford for their pursuers to catch up.

The mass of people parted, and the stairwell door appeared to their left.

"Are you ready to run?"

"Always."

He gave her a little push. "Now."

She was running before he'd even finished the word.

And the shout that followed picked up right where he left off. "After them."

EIGHT

Amy slammed her shin into the first step and nearly landed on her face, but a thick arm around her middle caught her in time. Fire shot up her leg and she hobbled for several strides, drawing on all of her training to ignore the pain and push through.

Jordan kept his hand on her, pushing her forward and holding her upright, somehow relieving a fraction of the pressure that released a burst of flame with every step.

Not that she needed his help. But she wasn't going to complain or pull away. Especially as they rounded the next flight and the entrance door crashed again. Booted feet slapped against the metal stairs. The din of each footstep made her heart pump a little harder until she was gasping for air.

It didn't help. There wasn't enough oxygen in the Amazon to slow her breathing to normal.

Her ears rang with the rush of adrenaline zipping through her system.

But there was also a quiet voice in her ear. "You've got this. Keep going."

It was soothing and calming, but he stopped at the same time as a hole burst out of the wall in front of her. Another quickly followed, and she ducked out of instinct.

"Nope. Keep going. As fast as you can."

Keep going. Keep going.

She just had to do it. She just had to keep her feet moving.

For Elaina.

The thought of what could be happening to her niece gave her another burst of energy. It was followed by a low chuckle in her ear. "Found something more, did you? Go. Go."

Grabbing the railing, she swung up to the next flight, only then realizing how damp her palms had become. But swiping them down her pants was guaranteed to throw off her rhythm, so she pushed through.

Suddenly the tenor of Jordan's voice changed. "This deck."

Which one was it? She'd lost count of how many they'd covered.

Jordan yanked open a door, pushed her through and rushed after her. Was there a chance that the noise of the door opening had been drowned out by the sound of the men behind them? She could only hope so, because the clambering had grown louder, proving that those men were gaining ground.

How could such big men move so quickly?

But there wasn't time to analyze. There was only time to look for a hiding place. And pray that the terrorists wouldn't fire into the crowd of sunbathers and revelers who packed the deck, soaking in the December rays.

Suddenly Jordan steered her into a small alcove. Lifeboats hung overhead, and for a moment, she thought he might boost her into one.

Instead, he pressed her against a wall of unforgiving wood and hovered over her, his face so close that she could feel his breath on her skin.

Her heart slammed into her rib cage as her mouth went dry, and she tried to look away, but there was nothing but him. Up and down. On each side. He surrounded her. Big and broad and ever the protector.

He made her feel small. Petite. Secure.

It was a feat few men had ever managed. Not when she wore a uniform. Not when she was five foot nine in her boots. Not when she normally carried a weapon most men had never fired.

She wished she didn't like the way he made her feel so much.

Even as she knew her body should be returning to normal after that run, her lungs continued pumping and her heart still beat rapidly. She bit into her suddenly quivering lip. But it wasn't just that that was shaking. Her hands and legs wouldn't stop trembling, either.

It was a lethal combination, fear, adrenaline and this strange awareness of the man in front of her.

He turned his head, likely searching for their pursuers, but it served only to highlight the line of his jaw. A day's worth of beard had grown there. It looked rough but somehow still soft. And before she realized it, she was reaching to run her fingers along it. Catching herself just in time, she yanked her hand back to her side as he turned to her.

"They're coming."

"Are we running again?" She hated that she sounded out of breath and confused.

He shook his head. "You saw those couples kissing on the deck?"

"Yes." She couldn't have missed them. Limbs tangled and lips pressed together, they'd refused to take their displays of affection out of the public eye.

And then it struck her, sending her stomach to her toes.

"You want to do that?"

"It's dark in here." His voice dropped until she couldn't tell if it was his tone or the words that scrubbed her nerves over a washboard and hung them out to dry. "We'll look like every other couple out there, like we just wanted a little privacy."

"Or we could take them head-on."

She didn't know why she spit it out so quickly. The idea of kissing Jordan wasn't *so* awful. She'd known him forever, and he wasn't bad-looking.

That's a big fat lie, and you know it, Amy Delgado.

Okay, he was better than not bad-looking. More like perfectly, classically, ideally handsome. Like he should have starred on one of those TV shows about special forces operatives turned cops.

But he'd also made a complete fool of her in front of his entire family a year ago, and then stood her up for the date that was supposed to be his apology.

"I'm going to kiss you. Right—" he peeked around the corner for a split second "—now."

Suddenly his hands cupped her face, tilted it back and his lips touched hers.

The entire world vanished.

If he'd surrounded her before, now she couldn't tell where she ended and he began. His calloused hands on her cheeks were surprisingly tender. While his lips remained gentle, there was an urgency in the connection.

It pulled at her, tugging her heart until it skipped a beat, making her forget how to even stand on her own feet.

Grappling with the wall behind her, she found nothing to hold on to, so she reached forward and grabbed the front of his black T-shirt. Her hands clenched into fists as she twisted the cotton fabric just to stay standing.

His arm slipped around her waist. An enormous hand spanned the width of her back as his fingers brushed against her spine. Pulling her closer, he paused for only the briefest breath, and she took advantage of it.

She couldn't seem to draw in enough air.

Her pulse raced and her head spun.

Beneath her grip on his shirt the beat of his heart felt strong and steady. It picked up speed with every thump until it was flying as fast as hers.

Then, without warning, he pulled away.

"They're past us now."

Amy's chest rose and fell like she'd just run a mile flat out, but Jordan wasn't out of breath. He gave no indication that the kiss had meant anything at all to him.

And her hands were still knotted into his shirt.

She dropped them, twisting them together behind her back and looking anywhere but at the perfect bow of his lips as she tried to figure out how she'd so easily forgotten they were even being chased. It didn't take long for her roaming gaze to meet his, and he popped one eyebrow in question.

But what he was asking remained unclear.

Are you all right?

Probably.

Was that okay?

Better than.

Do you want to do that again when no one's chasing us?

Definitely not. No. Absolutely never. Maybe.

Why was there even a question? The answer should be a given. She didn't like him. Everyone knew it. She hadn't even tried to pretend that they were on good terms, despite Neesha's repeated pleas for her to let go of the grudge.

But that was so much easier said than done. He'd humiliated her. And then, when she'd given him a chance to make up for it, he'd skipped their dinner date and hadn't even bothered trying to cover his lie.

Her fists clenched hard, and her blood rushed through her veins.

He'd claimed he was called up on a mission. He'd asked his teammate, his best friend, Zach, to call her to cancel the date. Of course he'd called her after she'd put on her new dress, applied thirteen coats of mascara, wrestled her hair into something resembling a French twist and sat on her couch for forty-five minutes.

And the rest of SEAL Team Fifteen? They were all conveniently still in San Diego. Probably right where Jordan had been that night, too.

In town with something better to do.

And she had spent that night alone and passed over.

She clenched her teeth so hard that her jaw ached, and she had to squeeze her eyes closed as she worked it out.

Jordan had treated her just like her dad used to. He'd made big promises—Disneyland, the zoo, even a trip to the mall to buy her a new teddy bear. And each time she'd sat on the couch and waited for him to arrive.

Every promise had been a lie. All of them.

And as a little girl craving her absent father's affections, they'd crushed her spirit.

But not anymore. She was a grown woman now, and she wasn't about to let Jordan do the same.

So why on earth would she think about kissing him again? For any reason?

Except that there had definitely been a connection, a spark, and she'd be lying if she tried to deny it.

She rolled her eyes at herself and leaned her head back against the wooden slats that made up the wall as he checked the deck again.

"They're definitely gone."

"Good."

"Did you recognize his voice? Was the American the same one you heard this morning?"

Her face pinched together as she thought about it. "I think so. But it was noisy in the service area. Still, how many Americans can be chasing me?"

His lips pursed, and he scraped his fingers along his beard, the low rasping a reminder that she hadn't taken advantage of maybe her only chance to do the same.

Don't think like that.

"Those men are looking for you. Now." Jordan pulled her from her wayward thoughts, his eyes crinkling at the corners as he frowned.

"You just figured that out, Somerton?" The question popped out before she even realized she wanted to ease his concern. She swatted at his arm, and like lightning he caught her fist in his own. Mouth suddenly dry, she croaked the rest. "I thought you were top of your class."

Without even acknowledging that he still held her hand captive, he said, "If they came for Elaina, they knew she was part of a wedding party."

A brick sank to the bottom of her stomach. Couldn't they just go back to the kissing? Even her own internal battle on that was better than trying to understand what these terrorists were after.

"Maybe they knew you were connected to Elaina."

She pinched her lips together. "They saw us together. Yesterday—was that just yesterday? When Eric Dean chased us. He saw us."

"Right. But what about before that?"

"Before the cruise?"

He nodded, and some of the mixed-up puzzle pieces in her mind began to fall into place. Or, at least, they fell into the correct piles. And sorting them might be half the battle.

"So what? They're not targeting Elaina because of me—it's Michael they're after."

Jordan released her hand and waved a finger in the air to keep her attention. "Stay with me on this. They captured Elaina because of Michael but they captured you, too. Why? Just because you were with her?"

"Right. Why else?"

"Because you could identify one of them."

Puzzle pieces scattered again, and she let out a slow breath. "I'm not following you."

"I assumed when you said you'd overheard a man say you could identify him that he thought you'd seen him when you and Elaina were taken last night."

"That's right."

He shook his head. "What if that's wrong?"

"Jordan, you're not making any sense."

"I'm sorry." He took a deep breath, and when he spoke again, his words were slow, almost methodical. "These men have shown they're not afraid to fire their weapons on this ship. They're clearly familiar with it and have hiding places. If you were just another hurdle between them and Elaina, why keep you around? Why not just kill you and get rid of your body?"

She blinked and sucked in a quick breath. "I have no idea."

"They're chasing you now. But what if they were always chasing you?"

A deep throbbing began behind her left eye and she pressed her fingers against it in a vain attempt to relieve some of the pressure, only remembering the bruise that swept across her face when she accidentally pressed too hard against the tender spot.

"What if Elaina wasn't the only target?" he said.

She held up one finger as her stomach took a spectacular nosedive. Pressing her other hand to her lips, she squinted at him and shook her head before asking a question she sure didn't want to know the answer to. "What makes you ask that?"

He answered it with another question of his own. "Was the man you heard in the storage closet one of the men that took you and Elaina last night?"

With a tight-lipped sigh, she shook her head. "How would I know? It was dark. I was hiding in a closet for most of it. And even when I came out, there weren't any lights on in the bedroom. I never got a good look at their faces."

"But did either of them have an American accent?"

Forcing herself to relive some of the worst moments of her life, she closed her eyes and let the scene play out. Big men. Loud. They crashed through the door. They spoke. One in broken English, the other was better at it. Their words played along, the soundtrack of her memory marked by Elaina's frightened breaths and the grasp of her little hands on Amy's arm as they sat on the floor of the closet.

But there was no born-and-raised American. None.

Her eyes flew open. "No. They weren't American. Not the ones last night." Her breath caught on a half sob as the truth struck home. "So how could I recognize someone who wasn't there?"

"Exactly. He thinks you'll recognize him from somewhere else."

"But where?"

Jordan could tell the exact moment Amy realized that this situation wasn't what they'd thought it was. Her face went pale, turning her gorgeous bronze glow into a faded painting, and her eyebrows nearly met in the middle of her forehead.

They were in trouble. And if it was tied to someone Amy would recognize from her work, then that meant it was DEA kind of trouble. But how did that connect to Michael and Elaina?

Amy was clearly lost in thought, pressing her fingers to her lips. The reminder that his lips had been there only a moment before was like a kick in the shin.

Was he going to remember that kiss—the way she'd clung to him and all of his senses had shut down except touch—every time he so much as looked at her lips?

No. No he was not. He had been trained better than that.

He was disciplined and controlled. And he would not lose his mind over a simple kiss with a woman who fit in his arms like she'd been made to be there. A woman who kept up with his every step. A woman smarter than he'd given her credit for.

She was tough and strategic and fearless. And when she twisted a strand of her hair around her finger, she was immensely feminine.

He looked away from the shiny lock of hair and tried not to remember how it had felt to thread his fingers through it only moments before.

She bit her lower lip, her white teeth pressing into the fullness there, and his head spun.

This was bad. So bad.

Concentrate. He only had to concentrate on the mission. And this Christmas cruise had certainly become one.

He cleared his throat, not trusting his voice, and tried to get his mind back on track. "So maybe this has something to do with both you *and* Michael."

"But what? Elaina is basically our only connection. I rarely talk with him these days, except to check on her or plan a visit." She crossed her arms over her chest, and her forehead wrinkled in a look that he was coming to recognize. "I mean, last night it sounded like you'd spent more time with him this year than I have."

The training that had eluded him a moment

before kicked in hard. He clamped his mouth closed and stared straight ahead.

She was asking why Michael, the Lybanian ambassador—not Michael, her brother-in-law—had recognized him.

And he couldn't say a word. He couldn't explain how bad he felt that he'd had to cancel their date because he'd been sent wheels up with another team in need of sniper. He wasn't free to talk about that mission or the Lybanian terrorist who had been threatening the lives of dozens of Americans and hundreds of Lybanian nationals.

"I'm sorry. I can't tell you why that is."

Her eyes narrowed, but her voice remained laid-back. "You say that a lot, don't you?"

"What?"

"That you can't talk about things."

There weren't words to explain. That mission and so many others were classified. He wasn't ever at liberty to talk outside of his team about where he'd been or where he was going.

And maybe as long as he had to keep his secrets, he'd never be able to convince her that he hadn't meant to stand her up that night.

Finally he shrugged. "It's always true."

She rolled her eyes and pushed away from the wall, cutting the distance between them in half. He held his ground and didn't back up or look away. But he forced himself not to think about how sweet she smelled this close to him.

"Listen," he said. "I get that for whatever reason you don't want to believe me, but—"

She raised her hand and slashed it in front of him. "We don't have time to hash out your lies and secrets."

Lies? He wanted to yell that he'd never lied to her. Ever.

But before he could, the phone in his pocket chirped.

Where are you? Have you seen Amy? She's supposed to be at the spa with us!!!! And she's not answering her room phone or returning my texts!!!!!!!

"It's Neesha. She seems upset. Lots of exclamation points and no emojis."

Amy's jaw dropped open, and she wrung her hands. "I forgot. It's the girls' day at the spa. She'll be worried about me."

"Yeah. Apparently she's been texting you."

Amy held up two empty, helpless hands. "My phone is gone."

"I know. I saw what was left of it."

"I...I need to see her. She has to know what's going on. It was one thing to keep her in the dark when we thought they were just after

Elaina. But now that we know they're looking to capture me, too… If they go after her looking for me, she won't be safe. She needs to know to protect herself." Amy took a step toward the deck and the sunlight that had shifted to reach its fingers into their little haven. "But…"

But they needed to find Elaina before whoever was arriving arrived.

She didn't even have to speak the words aloud. He knew they needed to split up—him to continue the search and her to warn Neesha. And if he couldn't tell her every story and reveal every secret, then at least he could continue where she wasn't able. Even if he'd much rather the two of them stayed together, and everything inside him screamed that he shouldn't let her out of his sight.

But he had to trust her. Because even when she'd been taken, she'd figured out a way get back to him.

He just prayed she wouldn't have to again.

"I'll go find Michael and get to the bottom of whatever you have in common—whatever would make them go after both of you."

The very thought gave him heartburn, and he pressed a fist against his chest to stem the flow. Usually he could control his body's reactions on a mission.

But he'd been able to control exactly nothing when it came to Amy Delgado.

"Okay. But you won't go after Elaina alone, right?"

"I won't. Where do you want to meet back up? When?"

He looked toward the bow and then the stern, picturing the ship's layout and trying to choose a relatively safe place. "What about Michael's second suite, where you were taken last night? There's no real reason for the tangos to come back to that spot. Plus there's still plenty of security buzzing around."

"All right. I'll see you there." She looked at her watch. "Forty-five minutes."

He nodded, peeked out of the alcove to be certain their pursuers were long gone and ushered her into the crowd.

His hand was still at the small of her back, and he looked down into her eyes. They nearly glowed beneath the sun's rays, but he couldn't even begin to read her thoughts. The relaxed line of her jaw was either a facade or a testament to her experience and strength.

Finally, they had to part ways. Before he knew what he was doing, he bent and pressed a kiss to her cheek, which was like satin. "Be careful."

Her eyes flashed with something, but it was

gone before he could read it. Then in a quiet voice she said, "You, too." She turned to go, but caught his arm before he'd fully turned away. "Forty-five minutes."

"I'll be there."

NINE

Jordan set off for the ambassador's current room, his senses on alert and a strange sensation in his chest. It felt oddly like fear, but not for himself. It wasn't about failing the mission—or really about the mission at all.

Something deep inside him wanted to give the feeling a name, but something more experienced promised that that would be a terrible mistake.

And then, before he knew it, his mother's face flashed before his eyes. He approached a row of deck chairs facing the swimming pool and nearly stumbled into them, pausing to catch his breath.

The memories were almost twenty-five years old. The knock on the door and the uniformed Charleston PD officer holding his hat in his hand. *Ma'am, I'm so sorry. There's been a shooting. Officer Somerton's been killed.*

His mom had dropped to the floor as if the

words had hit as hard as any bullet ever could, tears streaming down her face.

Jordan had hidden beneath the kitchen table. He'd pressed his hands over his ears so he wouldn't have to hear about the man who had tried to shoot his girlfriend but who had killed Jordan's father instead. His dad had been on a routine domestic disturbance call, and it had cost him his life.

At the time, all it meant to Jordan was that his dad wasn't going to come to his baseball game. They weren't going to the movies together. And he wasn't coming home. Ever.

But in the following months it had become clear that it meant so much more. It had meant his mom couldn't make it out of bed to feed him before school. Still wasn't out of bed when he came home. Forgot to wash herself and gave up trying to care for him.

That's when he began to realize that death could be so much more than sadness and grief. Sometimes death stole the living, too.

Jordan thanked God for Aunt Phyllis, who had swooped in all those years ago and given him a place in her loud and wild home, free from the grip of depression and the stink of the unwashed.

And that was why Jordan didn't get serious with girls.

He refused to be the reason a woman received a visit from a navy chaplain. He wouldn't ever put his wife through that.

So as long as he was on the teams, he wasn't going to have a wife. He couldn't.

No matter what this strange pressure in his chest suggested.

He took another shaky breath, glad he'd made it down a level and to the port side of the ship without incident. Somewhere between the alcove and the cabin, he'd gotten lost in memories of his mother and in questions he'd never asked himself before. Was the trade-off worth it? Would he rather be a SEAL than be in love?

And there was no doubt in his mind that Amy was the reason he was even contemplating such thoughts.

If ever there was a woman worth giving up everything for, she would be the one.

This train of thought did him no good, and he tried to excise it by pounding on the door of room. But as soon as he realized how ominous that knock sounded, he cringed. Maybe he should have employed the secret knock Amy had used before.

As it was, the light on the other side of the peephole went dark for a moment, then a low voice asked, "What do you want?"

"It's Jordan." Not that Pete hadn't seen for himself. "I need to speak to the ambassador."

All was silent for a long minute, and Jordan passed the time by taking a moment to really survey the row of rooms that lined the hallway and covering a jaw-cracking yawn.

Scrubbing his hand down his face, he pushed fatigue to the back of his brain and tried to focus on the layout before him. A potted palm tree in the corner was decked with white twinkle lights in a nod to the holiday season. And every door had a small wreath attached to it.

A twenty-foot evergreen dressed in its finest ribbons and bows had filled the grand foyer. He rolled his eyes just thinking about it because ships were not supposed to have foyers. They were supposed to have flight decks and mags for storing weapons and ammunition.

But Neesha had wanted to be married on a Christmas cruise, so she'd chosen a floating ship of frivolity. Only it wasn't quite so frivolous now.

He stared at the dancing lights on the tree for another second before he realized that one of the lights never wavered. And it wasn't the same soft white as the others. It was more yellow and unblinking.

Strolling toward it, he nodded to a gray-haired couple holding hands and whispering as they wandered down the passageway. As he drew closer to the plant, he realized why the light wasn't flashing. It wasn't part of the decorative strand at all. It was attached to the wall about at his eye level.

A security camera.

Well, how many of these were hidden around the ship? And what had the security team seen that they hadn't shared?

"Petty Officer?"

He turned toward the ambassador, who leaned warily out of his doorway. "Just looking at the tree," Jordan said as he marched back to Torres. "I need to speak with you about Amy."

"Has she been taken again?"

"No." At least, he hoped not. He told himself that she'd be fine getting to Neesha. And if she ran into trouble, she could handle herself. "But I think that whoever took your daughter has a connection to Amy, as well."

Torres waved him inside and pointed to the striped sofa in the living room. "How can that be? I'm sure this is all related to those death threats I was getting in Washington. Amy had nothing to do with them. She didn't even know about them." Plopping onto the opposite couch, he ran his fingers through his hair until it stood on end. "Has there been any sign of Elaina?"

"No. We scoured the service area near the

kitchen, and there was no indication she'd been there. But we did run into someone who we believe was one of the attackers. Someone with an American accent. It seems he thinks Amy can recognize him."

"But Amy's okay?"

Jordan squinted. "She's fine. She's checking on Neesha and the bridesmaids." Running his palms down the legs of his jeans, he took a breath and tried to find the right questions to ask. "Why would someone targeting your daughter be afraid that Amy could recognize them?"

Torres shrugged one shoulder. "I have no idea. Could it be a coincidence?"

"No." He didn't bother with explanations. He also didn't bother believing in coincidences. It never paid off.

"Then I have no idea. I hadn't seen Amy in months until this cruise. We talked maybe six times all year, and that was mostly because I answered the phone when she was calling for Elaina."

"Mostly?" Jordan latched on to the innocuous word. "When was it not that?"

Michael's face puckered, and he stared at the ceiling. "When…when…when I met her team to thank them for the drug bust."

"Drug bust?" Jordan's stomach clenched and

twisted, and he rubbed suddenly antsy hands together. Why had no one thought to mention a drug bust?

"Amy's team was working a drug smuggling case. Big shipments were coming through crates at the San Diego harbor—almost four hundred pounds of heroin."

"So, why were you there?" Jordan asked.

"The shipments originated in Lybania, and several of the men detained with the shipment were high-level Lybanian terrorists." Michael leaned his elbows on his knees, seemingly hesitant to share more, but after a look at Jordan, he continued, "The State Department thought it would be helpful for me to be there. After they were booked, I stopped by to thank the DEA team for their hard work. Amy and I spoke for about three minutes."

Did he even hear the words he was speaking? "You just said that Amy stopped four hundred pounds of heroin from hitting US streets."

Torres nodded.

"And you don't think someone was mad that almost three hundred million dollars of funding for their terrorist activities just went down the tubes?" Jordan had to struggle to keep his voice calm. Yelling wouldn't do any good. "Do you know what kind of arms a terrorist cell in Lybania could buy with that kind of money?"

Realization washed over Torres in visible and audible ways. First his face turned white and then he groaned. Finally he stood and paced the confines of the room. "Did they take my Elaina because of Amy? To get back at her?"

"I don't think so." Jordan stood so he didn't have to look up at the ambassador but stayed rooted in his spot between the couches. "But I wouldn't ignore the connection to that bust, either."

Through his hands covering his face, the ambassador said, "What are we going to do?"

They needed help. But this cruise ship—an older one in the fleet—wasn't equipped with cell phone service. Calling from the room phone could alert the terrorists, too. And even if they could call for help, there was no guarantee that a ship was anywhere nearby. It could take hours to scramble help.

And they might not have hours.

"We need to get help and fast."

Torres nodded, his face grim with understanding. "Maybe they're not watching you?"

Jordan didn't hold out much hope, but he pulled his phone from his pocket, swallowing the dread that came with what he saw. "I'm not connected to the internet." He had been. Just fifteen minutes ago, he'd gotten the message from Neesha. But now his internet connection had been severed. And he'd wager that was the case for everyone else on the ship. They'd been cut off.

Torres snatched up his phone and confirmed the same. "I checked my email earlier, but now nothing."

But why do it now? Why would the terrorists alert everyone on the ship to their presence? And if they were finally ready to play their hand openly, what would that mean for Elaina?

He couldn't stand still a moment longer and paced the length of the sofa. It took exactly two and a half steps to go from armrest to armrest, then he spun and repeated his motions. At least it was movement, and maybe it would be enough to get his brain going, to think through what needed to be done, what he should do next.

"How helpful has the captain been to you?" he asked.

"Very." Torres drew his dark eyebrows into a single line, and he scratched at his chin. "He's given me three different cabins."

But somehow the terrorists still knew where to find Elaina.

"He sent a security officer by here a few times to check on the ambassador, too."

Jordan nearly jumped when Pete piped up. He'd nearly forgotten the big man was standing in the corner. He wasn't the most talkative or quick thinking of bodyguards. But he did seem to care about Michael and Elaina, which was a key part of the job description.

"And he offered me free use of his office and his secure phone," Torres added.

"Which you can't use again without alerting someone to that fact—if the phone is even working."

Torres looked up from where his gaze had been trained on the floor, his eyes darting in Pete's direction and then to Jordan. "You think that's been taken out, too? Have we been cut off? Why now?"

"Good question." And there was only one answer he could come up with. "I believe something is going to happen that will absolutely draw the attention of everyone on this ship, and they can't afford for word to get out about what's happening."

"But if we're cut off, how can we get help?"

Jordan shook head and stared at the ceiling. "The cruise line will be tracking us, and if we're sent off course for any unexplained reason, they'll alert the Coast Guard."

"But what if we're not off course?" Pete asked.

"We might be. We can pray that we will be. If I can find someone to help us, I will.

Until then, you need to stay safe until we reach St. Thomas."

Sure, that sounded well and good, but he was still unarmed and facing a threat he didn't fully understand. More terrorists kept popping up. Elaina was still missing, and he couldn't afford for her to wind up in the middle of some cross fire.

But he had a suspicion that the hidden security cameras might have some useful information.

Marching toward the door, he stopped only when Torres called his name. "Where are you going?"

"I need to check in with the staff captain. I have some security questions for him."

"What should I do?" The ambassador's voice wobbled just a hint, betraying the diplomatic facade he so carefully kept in place.

"Stay put." Jordan looked back just before swinging open the door. "And pray."

TEN

Amy pulled Neesha into a hug, but that didn't stop the bride from squealing in front of the crowded spa. "Where have you been? You're two hours late, and I've been texting you all morning. We've already gotten our toes done." She held up her hand and wiggled her fingers. "And we're about to get our nails done. Sit. Sit."

Neesha was at least a few rings outside of bridezilla territory, but that didn't mean she didn't know what she wanted and where she wanted her attendants at all times on this cruise.

One of the staff members, wearing a purple smock and a kind smile, put her arm around Amy's back. "We'll get you taken care of."

"No. I can't stay. I have to meet—"

Neesha's pursed lips turned into a true frown. "What do you mean you can't stay? This is my wedding cruise. I want my best friends surrounding me, getting pampered with me. The wedding is in two days. Don't you want to look your best?"

"I do but…"

The eyes of the five other bridesmaids followed her every move, and they hung on her every word. This was not the time or the place to explain about the kidnapping. But convincing Neesha to step away from the spa would be almost impossible.

"Wait, you said you have to meet up with someone." Neesha's eyes grew wide, long lashes fluttering with excitement. "Did you meet someone? I told you it could happen anywhere."

"No." And then her memory flashed every sweet sensation of Jordan's kiss, and her entire body shivered.

"Who is it?" Camille, another one of the bridesmaids, called from the chair where the last clear coat of polish was drying on her toenails.

Meredith, who was sitting next to Camille, hollered, "I think it's that French guy who's been running around the deck in his Speedo."

Moans and groans flooded the spa, with even the employees chuckling in agreement.

Amy offered a half grin but shook her head. Even if she wasn't involved in a life-or-death mission, she still would never be interested in the French guy in need of a larger bathing suit and some heavy-duty sunscreen, if his wrinkled leather skin was any indication. Jordan was about the opposite of the rotund man.

"Very funny, Mer. Ha. Ha."

All the girls giggled again. "Then tell us who it is."

She had a sudden urge to lie and say that she was meeting up with Elaina. But lies never solved anything, so she closed her eyes, hunched her shoulders and prepared for the worst. "I have to meet Jordan."

The squeals were deafening.

"Really?"

"Oh, Amy! He's *so* handsome!"

"It's about time. The two of you have been circling each other forever."

"Does this mean he's off the market?"

It was Neesha's voice that rose above all of the others. "You've finally forgiven him, haven't you?" She grabbed Amy's hands and squeezed hard. "I told you he's wonderful. He's such a good man. He really is. He just made some dumb choices. He never wanted to hurt you. But now that's in the past, and the two of you together would be—"

"We are not together." Amy had to cut her off. She didn't want to hear more about Jordan's finer qualities. She'd been seeing them firsthand for the last eighteen hours or so, and she didn't need another voice in her head suggesting that she might have overreacted to his rejection.

Maybe her grudge had more to do with her dad than with Jordan.

But that didn't mean she was ready to let it go.

She tried to plaster a consoling smile into place. "We've been…" She needed a word. Anything to describe what was actually happening rather than the images in their minds. The trouble was, if they were picturing them kissing, so was she.

Focus, Delgado. This is about keeping Neesha safe.

"We've been working on an assignment together. Nothing more."

"An assignment?" Neesha recoiled in surprise that quickly turned to anger. "You said you took time off. Jordan promised that he was on leave. This is my wedding, and I hate to play the bride card, but this is all about me. For at least two more days. Understand?" Her tone never rose, and her words were unfailingly even. But there was a steel in them that must run in the family. She'd heard the same from Jordan when he'd insisted on sticking by her side.

"I know. But something's come up." Amy tugged on her arm. "Can we talk in private? For just a minute."

Neesha looked over her shoulder at a row of

bewildered faces, and Amy wished she could explain it to them all. But prewedding stress was high and the chances of all of them keeping their calm very, very low.

With a curt nod, Neesha acquiesced, shuffling behind her in flimsy oversize flip-flops. They found a dark corner of the spa, a luscious purple curtain blocking the view of the rest of the amenities.

Amy didn't dance around the subject. "Elaina's been kidnapped."

Neesha's mouth went wide like she was going to scream, and Amy pushed her hand against it.

"Don't. We can't draw attention."

After a long pause, Neesha nodded her agreement. Amy removed her hand, and Neesha stood like a stone for another silent second. And then the floodgates opened. "What do you mean? I just saw her last night. She was fine."

"I know. But they came after her last night. I was with her. And they took me, too."

Neesha's mouth opened and closed, but no sound emerged. Her eyes turned liquid, and she pressed her hands to her face.

"I'm okay," Amy reassured her. "I got away. But they're still looking for me."

"Who would do that? Why would anyone come after you? Where could they possibly take her on this ship? There isn't anywhere to go."

She made a great point. But it seemed that someone knew a secret spot that she and Jordan hadn't found because Elaina had vanished practically right in front of them. Neesha asked questions that Amy couldn't answer, so she skirted them with what she did know.

"Jordan and I are working on it, but in the meantime, I think the men who are after me know I'm part of your wedding party."

Tears leaked down Neesha's cheeks, and she swiped at them with her knuckles. "Are they going to come after me or Rodney or the girls?"

Amy had to find the kindest truth. "If you stay cautious, I'm sure you'll be fine. But I wanted you to know so that you'd be on your guard."

Neesha's lower lip trembled, as she stared in the direction of the rest of the wedding party. Amy could practically see the scenarios playing out in her mind. Her wedding ruined, her friends injured—or worse.

This wasn't the way any girl dreamed of starting the rest of her life, and Amy could do nothing but ask her friend to put on her big-girl pants and face it head-on.

"I need you to be careful, okay?"

Neesha nodded.

"Have you noticed anyone hanging around?

A guy who's not part of the party? Someone who's there wherever you go."

"No. Nothing like that. But I've been a little…"

"Distracted." Amy filled it in for her. "It's okay. Just please don't go anywhere alone. If you can stay close to Rodney, that would be best. You need to stay alert. Be aware of your surroundings. And please don't say anything. To anyone."

Neesha blinked rapidly, her arms circling her stomach as though she could somehow comfort herself. "Not even Rodney?"

"You can tell Rodney, but just him. Make sure he knows to keep it to himself, and don't discuss it anywhere where you might be overheard. We can't afford to tip them off that we're coming after Elaina."

Neesha nodded slowly. "Okay, what if I see something? I should text you?"

"My phone was… I lost it."

Neesha let out a quick breath. "Okay." Then suddenly she grabbed Amy by the shoulders and pulled her in for a hug that nearly stole her breath. "You be careful, all right? I have to break in a new husband, and I don't have time to break in a new best friend, too."

Amy held on tight to the woman she'd known

for most of her life, savoring the comfort. "I will. I promise. I've got to go."

She slipped out of the spa without passing the rest of the wedding party and stalked down a hall toward the elevator closest to the meeting spot. She kept her chin down but eyes alert. Her pace was even and steady, but she was always ready to take off at a flat run if she needed to.

But she didn't need to be quite so wary. She hardly saw anyone in the hallways, and those she did rushed by her, their swim bags swishing and sandals clacking along the carpet. They barely gave her a second look as they rushed to soak in the vitamin D on the upper deck, the warm and abundant sunshine a rarity for half the world this time of year.

A glance at her watch told her that she would be a few minutes late if she didn't hurry, so she picked up her pace the last hundred yards, but even as she rounded the last bend, she saw that she'd beaten Jordan. Maybe he was running late, too.

Except she'd never known him to run late. He was exceedingly punctual.

A year ago, they'd been on the same flight from San Diego to Charleston to celebrate Neesha and Rodney's engagement. He'd offered to give her a lift to the airport, and she'd been happy to accept. He'd said he'd arrive at oh-seven-hundred, and the clock in her entry-way was sounding the first chime of the seven o'clock hour when he knocked on her door.

She'd been ready.

That was military time. On time and ready to roll.

He was either on time…or he didn't come at all, like the night of their would-be date.

As the second hand on her watch ticked by the minutes, a band around her lungs began to pull tight. She paced in front of the repaired cabin door, attempting to entertain herself by trying to figure out how long it had taken a carpenter to put another frame into place and reset the door.

That distraction lasted about twenty seconds. But she kept pacing, kept her feet moving and her eyes ever watchful.

As minutes turned into quarter hours, her heart picked up, playing out all the evils he could have stumbled upon. Or worse, maybe he'd decided to go it alone. Without her. Didn't he understand that she was an asset rather than a liability?

Her stomach churned, anger boiling low and endless as she imagined his face, so smug about leaving her behind.

Silly Amy. Didn't she know that his plans didn't include her?

Fists clenched so tightly that they shook, she nearly kicked the new doorjamb. She'd fallen for his false promises again. She'd expected him to follow through. She'd let herself hope that the past didn't define the present.

Stupid Amy.

As she stomped down the hall, even the lights seemed to be tinged with red and she fought the urge to push the too-cheerful-for-its-own-good palm tree to the floor.

She didn't hear the other body approaching from around the corner, and she slammed into him at full force. Big hands immediately grabbed her shoulders, the only thing that kept her from falling on her rear end as she bounced off his chest.

"Amy!" Jordan kept his hands in place and ducked to look her directly in the eye. Then suddenly he pulled her into a tight hug.

"Get off me." She tried to push away his arms, but it was a little like taking a fly swatter to a mountain.

When he pulled back, his eyes burned with something she couldn't name, and immediately his head whipped around, his gaze darting into every corner. "What's wrong? What happened?"

"You—" She couldn't keep the tremor out of her voice, anger taking over even her vocal chords. "You said you'd meet me here. And then you took off without me. You left me."

He let out a quick breath and suddenly brushed a thumb across her cheek, leaving a damp trail in its wake. Even her tear ducts were rebelling. Perfect.

"I'm sorry I'm late."

"*Sorry*. It's always sorry with you. Why not just show up when you say you're going to? Then an apology wouldn't be necessary."

He rubbed his knuckles across the top of his head. "I deserve that. I know I don't have the best track record with you, but I promise, I have a good reason for being late."

"Hmph." She couldn't get any more past the lump that popped up in her throat. Relief had begun to mix with the fury, and it was producing a whole new set of emotions that she didn't have the time or patience to analyze.

"I did some exploring. And do you know what I found?"

Arms crossed over her stomach and toe tapping, she shook her head. "I have no idea. Do I care?"

"I think you're going to." One corner of his mouth tipped up as he pulled one of her hands free and took off toward a back set of elevators.

"Where are we going? What are you doing?"

He stopped suddenly and pointed. "See that light?"

"Of course." She barely gave it a glance, but the pleased look on his face couldn't be ignored. She looked again. And her heart picked up its pace.

"That's a camera."

"And they're all over. Including in the passageway outside the ambassador's original suite. I checked. And then there's this one." He pointed in a line from the camera all the way down the hall past the door she'd just been pacing in front of.

Was it possible that the cameras had captured Elaina's kidnapping? Could they track the movements of the kidnappers from here to the girl's current location? This could be the break they needed. As long as someone on the inside hadn't tampered with the footage.

After all, someone had definitely failed to mention the cameras before now. But it was the first hope of finding Elaina she'd had in hours. And she'd take it.

Anger vanished in that moment, and she flung her arms around his waist, squeezing tight, burying her nose into his chest. "Thank you."

He tipped her head back so he could meet her

gaze full on. "I'm going to do everything in my power to get her back and to keep you safe. I promised. Can you trust me to do that?"

He didn't know what he was asking of her, and she pulled all the way out of the embrace.

She wasn't going to make false promises, either. "I'll try."

"Thank you." Then without preamble, he grabbed her hand and tugged. "Let's go find those videos."

She chased him as they made their way through the ship's maze, finally popping up at the security office. He banged on the door, which rattled under the pressure.

The tinny voice of a security officer came through a box beside the door. "Can I help you?"

"This is Petty Officer Jordan Somerton. I want to speak to the staff captain. Immediately."

Whether it was the unyielding tone of his voice or the intimidating width of his shoulders, she couldn't be sure. But one way or another they were ushered into the office and given chairs at a desk within minutes.

The staff captain had yet to make an appearance but one of the security guys—he'd introduced himself as Bo—kept staring at Jordan. "You're in the navy?" His voice was hushed with wonder.

He nodded slowly, but Amy knew right where this was going.

"You ever meet a SEAL?" Bo asked.

Jordan produced a slow smile as they settled in front of a computer screen. "I've met a few."

She shot him a look that she hoped communicated that this was not the time for modesty—or for teasing men who might be able to help them find and secure Elaina.

He shrugged and finally continued. "I am a SEAL."

Bo's eyes got bigger than dinner plates. "No way. Really? Do you have a tattoo?"

Only Amy heard the tiny, exasperated sigh he released. She nudged him with her knee. "Of course he does."

After Jordan rolled up his sleeve and showed off his trident tattoo, the kid was in awe and eager to please. "Where do you want to start?" he asked.

Jordan made sure that Amy was settled in with a prime view of the screen before nodding at Bo. "Last night. Around twenty-three-thirty. Can you start in the hallway outside the ambassador's room?"

Bo asked for the room number, and then punched the information into the computer until the electronic files popped up. The video was black and white and grainy, and it showed other passengers walking to and from their rooms. There was a distinct influx when the comedy show let out, couples and families returning to their beds. And then they saw the ambassador leave his room, trailed by his bodyguard. A few minutes later Jordan left, too.

The hall was clear for several long minutes.

"Can you fast-forward it?"

"Sure." Bo did as asked, and the counter clock sped forward thirty minutes before two figures suddenly appeared. They were big and brawny, and the sight of them made Amy's stomach roll.

They watched in silence as the goons took out the door, and even though Amy knew what was happening inside that room, she held her breath. It was like wishing that a novel would turn out differently upon the second read. It didn't happen. But it didn't keep her from hoping for just a moment.

And just when she realized that her hands were clenched in her lap, Jordan reached for them. "It's okay," he whispered.

If Bo heard, he said nothing, and Amy let herself accept the comforting touch for a long moment. It didn't mean anything. But she sure was glad for the weight of his hand on hers when the two men emerged, one carrying a wiggling, lashing Elaina, a white cloth pressed to her mouth. The other carried her own limp form.

It was an oddly out-of-body experience to watch something happen to her that she couldn't remember, and the bruise on the side of her face throbbed.

Elaina got a good kick into her abductor's stomach, and he grunted, nearly dropping the girl before whatever drug they'd used in the cloth began to take effect and her limbs turned listless.

"Looks like Elaina learned something from her aunt," Jordan said.

Warmth rushed up her neck, but she said, "Of course. Delgado women aren't pushovers." She focused her attention back on Bo. "Can you track them?"

Bo frowned, his skinny pale neck revealing even more veins. "I think so. They've gone into corridor 7C." He flipped to another video, and sure enough, the two men were walking straight toward the camera, their faces clearly visible, if somewhat pixelated.

Jordan shot her a careful look. "Do you recognize either of them?"

Amy shook her head. "I think the one carrying me, the one with the limp—I think he's the one I tackled. The one who hit me." Covering her ear and the side of her face with her hand, she tried to forget how bad that bruise was going to look in a few short days. It hadn't turned dark purple yet or Neesha would have been all over it. "But I don't know him from anywhere else."

They tracked the men through several flights and multiple passages. Several times they lost sight of the men in hallways without cameras, but with some trial and error they found them again. Bo moved so quickly that she lost track of where they were looking. But the men on-screen seemed to know back ways and deserted corridors. Even in the middle of the night it was strange that they hadn't run into anyone.

Unless...

Maybe they were getting help from the same person who helped Eric Dean escape.

Suddenly the men nodded at each other and the one carrying Elaina veered down another hallway.

"Follow the girl," Amy ordered.

"Yes, ma'am."

And then suddenly the man wasn't alone. Another man, shorter, his hair lighter, stepped into the frame. He took Elaina and clamped his hand over the rag at her mouth. But just before he disappeared into the darkness, he looked right into the camera.

Her heart slammed to a stop and then started up again, painful and abrasive.

"Wait. Can you pause it? Rewind."

Bo cued it up to his face.

"That's the man who was chasing us earlier when..." Jordan's voice tapered off, and for a second, he looked mildly uncomfortable.

In any other circumstance, Amy would have laughed at Jordan. But now all she could see were the bitter features of the man on the screen. His nose had been broken at least once, and his lips were so thin they were barely there. He scowled as though he'd forgotten—or never learned—how to smile. And his beady little eyes spoke volumes.

Her insides were tied up in a knot and those ridiculous puzzle pieces were beginning to make a picture she could understand.

"I know that man."

Jordan nearly swallowed his tongue. He shouldn't have been surprised. He wasn't, really.

But the softness and certainty in Amy's voice made the hair on his arms stand on end. He wanted—no, needed—to hear it all. But first they needed a little bit of privacy.

"Bo, where does he go after this?"

Bo shook his head when the man stepped out of range of that camera. "I can't follow him past this point. We don't have any cameras in that deep."

"Where is he right there?"

Bo pulled up a map of the ship and showed

them. "It's a stairwell that leads to the back side of the kitchen."

Jordan caught Amy's eye, and he knew she was thinking the same thing. They'd been on the wrong side of the kitchen. They'd been so close to Elaina, but they'd missed her because there were two kitchen exits. Not one.

Jordan reached out his hand and shook Bo's with a quick pump. "Thank you for your help. The teams could use good men like you."

The kid's blue eyes shone like someone had lit a candle within him. "You serious, man? You think I could do it? I could be a SEAL?"

"Only you can answer that. But for what it's worth, I think you'd stand a real shot."

Jordan grabbed Amy's hand, tugged her toward the exit and left Bo to ponder that statement.

They still hadn't seen Xavier, but there was no time to wait and no one with enough authority to send help with them. They were probably better off without it. Some of these security guards were eager to offer their services but severely under-trained—like Bo. Some were downright apathetic—like Cortero the night before. And not being able to rely on the man beside you was worse than having no one there.

Good thing he had Amy.

He smiled at her, and she responded with

one of her own, tense but hopeful. And his insides tripped.

He liked her. He liked spending time with her. He liked that he could trust her. He liked how strong and independent and fierce she was. And he liked how she'd spoken to her niece at the party the night before. Soft, calming, compassionate words. She could take down an entire drug ring in one breath and comfort a frightened child in the next.

And he'd be lying if he pretended he hadn't noticed how beautiful she was while doing it all. The highlights in her dark hair shone in the sun like a halo. Even on the run, out of breath and scared, her skin glowed a deep bronze, and her brown eyes sparkled. And when she smiled— well, it wasn't safe to think about those lips for too long because that just reminded him of their kiss and how much he wanted another one.

He wasn't in love with her or anything ridiculous like that. But…but she made him wish his personal rules were different.

Maybe for the first time.

They reached a semiprivate corner outside the security office and he stopped, turning to assess her current state. The stunned expression had been replaced by one of determination.

"Why are we stopping?" she asked. "Let's get going."

"In a minute. First, tell me—who is that man?"

"His name is Bruno Stein. He's an American connected to the Lybanian drug ring that my team took down this summer."

"I thought maybe he was connected to that. Michael told me that he'd seen your team after that. It's the only plausible connection. But what happened in that operation that would set off this level of an attack? What did you do to make them so angry?"

She raised an eyebrow in question. "You mean besides confiscating four hundred pounds of heroin?"

He nodded.

"We arrested their leader, General Abkar." Her lips formed a tight line for a long second. "And I think they're going to try to use Elaina as a bargaining chip to get him back."

ELEVEN

Jordan raced after Amy down the passageways that they'd only seen before on the security monitor. They bumped into packs of other people on the upper decks, but as they moved into the bowels of the ship, the crowds thinned, eliminating much of their cover.

So long as there were other people around, they weren't quite as conspicuous to anyone who might be watching for them. And it was unlikely that Stein and the other terrorists were just milling around in crowds.

With each level they passed, down each ladder, the chances of running into Stein grew. So did the knot in Jordan's stomach.

By the time they reached the deck above the kitchen, he could nearly hear his own heart pounding. His shoulders were tense, his neck already stiff in anticipation of what was to come.

Even though he really had no idea what to expect.

Were they entering a swarm or a hive?

Were armed men running around without order or position, or did everyone have a place and a job?

If it was the latter, their best option was to take the men out one at a time, commandeer their weapons and hide the bodies.

If the former, their best option was prayer. Men without orders were unpredictable and often careless. They shot first and rarely bothered to ask questions later. And they tended to blend into a crowd, making them harder to identify as the enemy.

But either way, he was ready for a fight.

"Jordan?" Amy's voice was barely a whisper as they reached a corner. "Do you hear that?"

He'd been so caught up in making a plan that he'd missed whatever she'd heard. He held still, listening carefully.

All was silent save for the crashing of metal pots and pans in the kitchen below. The deck between them muffled the words, but the cries of busy line cooks and demanding chefs wouldn't be denied.

He nodded toward the floor, asking Amy if that's what she'd heard.

She mouthed *no* and pointed her chin toward the corner.

His pulse kicked up a notch, sweeping adrenaline through him.

He pointed to himself and then to the corner.

Sinking to the ground, he crawled to a better vantage point and peeked around the corner. He wouldn't be easily visible this low to the ground, so he pushed himself a little farther into the opening to get a full view.

Two men stood by the entrance to the stairs, trying—and failing—to look casual. Maybe it was the Glock hanging in the hand of the one on the left or what looked like an Uzi conspicuously tucked into the jacket of the other. Either way, they were decidedly not casual.

And they had a straight shot down a short passageway with no obstacles—or opportunities for cover—in their way.

If Jordan tried to take them head-on, he'd be hit. Without question.

And he couldn't risk Amy suffering the same.

Wiggling back to Amy, he stood and shook his head. "Not good. Two armed men—but I don't recognize them. No cover. It's a straight shot, and no way to get to them except from behind. Only that's the stairwell we're trying to get to. We need a better angle."

She chewed on her lower lip for a long second, her eyes gazing overhead. "If we play a couple that's lost…"

The image of her arm wound around his and fingers threaded between his own, her eyes gazing up at him adoringly, flashed through his mind and delivered a punch to his throat.

That didn't sound bad. At all.

But what if these men were shoot-first-ask-questions-later kind of guys?

"No."

Her lips pursed, eyes narrowing in on him. "How about if we separate them?"

"And how do you suggest we do that?"

A slow smile spread across her lips. "I have an idea, so just go with me on this."

A band around his lungs cinched tight, and he grabbed at her arm. "Don't try to be a hero, Delgado. There's a lot at stake here."

She didn't back down. If anything, she took a step toward him. "Like my niece."

"And she needs you alive." His voice rose, and he had to swallow the fear that was already beginning to take root. "We all need you alive."

"And I will be. But for now, I need you to trust me."

"I do."

Oh, Lord, what is she thinking? Don't let her get herself killed.

Amy took a deep breath and tried to give Jordan a reassuring smile as she pushed him out of sight into another hallway. "Say put," she breathed.

He nodded, but then shook his head. "If you scream, I'm coming to get you. Understood?"

"Sure." She dismissed it with flippant wave of her hand, but everything inside her seized up because she *did* understand. This was not a lukewarm promise, and she didn't have any doubt that he'd follow through.

This was the first time she'd been so certain of any man since her dad stopped bothering to show up.

But this was not the time for reflection.

This was the time for action. And pretending.

Flipping her hair over, she gave it a good shake, then pinched a bit of color into her cheeks and bit her lips to turn them red.

God, help me.

And then she let the role begin. "Jason! Jason Burke, you come out here right now." She paused and made her panic rise, using it to fuel the character she was playing. Not too difficult when she was about to turn a corner to face two armed men. But this had to be realistic, like she had lost her charge, but not like she was ready for a weapons fight.

She ran along the carpet, hugging the wall, then stopped and screamed again. "Jason, if you don't come out right now, you're not getting any dessert." Forcing out a loud sob, she prayed they'd buy the whole scenario. "Jason."

Blood pumping hard, she rounded the corner and stopped in her tracks.

Act surprised. She had to act surprised.

Her mouth dropped open, and she batted her lashes at them, wishing she'd had enough time that morning to put on at least one coat of mascara. "Have you seen a little boy? He's six, and he has a habit of running off, but if his parents find out I've lost him again, I'm going to be in so much trouble."

The two big men stood nearly paralyzed in front of a dark wood door. Neither blinked at her for what felt like an eternity, and their paralysis seeped into her, rooting her feet and her facial features for too long.

Her gaze couldn't seem to stray from the Glock that hung a little too loosely in the hand of the man on the left. He squeezed his finger against the trigger, and her heart stopped.

This wasn't working. But she was in too deep to back out now.

Play the part. She had to play the part.

Sucking in a stabilizing breath, she flipped her hair over her shoulder and smiled again. "Have you seen him?" Holding a hand at waist level, she tried again. "Brown hair, green shirt?"

Slowly the man who was clearly covering a submachine gun under his jacket shook his head. "We've seen no one."

Amy forced herself to burst into tears—not a terribly difficult task given the rush of emotion thundering through her. "He said—" She sobbed loudly and stumbled toward them. "He said that he was going to play a game, but now he's hiding and I can't find him. And we were supposed to meet his parents twenty minutes ago."

Glock guy nodded slowly, like he understood her predicament but had no idea how to help.

Good.

"I think he might have locked himself in the men's bathroom." She covered her face with one hand, leaving just enough of a view to watch their reactions. "And *I* can't go in after him." She wailed hard at the end of it.

Please, please let this work.

Lybanians weren't known for treating women well in their country. But it was a truth universally acknowledged that men didn't know how to handle a crying woman.

They remained silent, and then suddenly Glock guy reached behind him and tucked his weapon into the back of his waistband. "Fine. I will look."

"Really?" She tipped back her head and shot him her best impression of a pageant queen smile—so toothy and bright that it made her cheeks ache. "It's just around the corner. I can't thank you enough."

Thinking twice about putting a hand on him, she waved in the direction where she'd left Jordan.

Lybanian custom dictated that women walk at least a pace behind any man in their group, and she quickly fell into place. He didn't even seem to notice.

As soon as they were outside the view of machine-gun man, she slipped her hand beneath his jacket and pulled his gun free.

Oh, man, it felt good to have a weapon in her hand again.

He turned, rage on his face and mouth open ready to scream. But she held the Glock in both hands, arms straight and level with his nose.

"How dare—"

Her heart leaped to her throat as she pressed her finger against the trigger. It always did.

But before it could fully engage, an elbow flew out of nowhere, connecting to his face. The crunch of bone as his nose shattered made her cringe, and Glock guy—or rather previously Glock guy—crumpled to the ground, an unconscious form covered in crimson streams.

Her gaze shot to Jordan, who stood over him, a satisfied grin in place. His smile turned into a half frown as he stared at her. "You okay?"

Her hands trembled slightly, but she shoved them behind her. It was just the action kicking too much adrenaline through her system. Shaky limbs were pretty normal for her in the aftermath of situations like this. "Good."

"One down." He nodded to the motionless man on the floor. "You want to get the other or want me to?"

Holding out the gun, she said, "You're the sniper."

His hands dwarfed the pistol as he took it from her. "Be right back."

She held her breath, waiting for the pop of gunfire. But it didn't come. Instead a loud voice demanded, "What are you—"

"Drop it." Jordan's voice was lethal, terrifying. And there was an immediate clatter on the floor. It was muffled by the carpet, but she knew without a doubt that machine-gun man had surrendered.

For a long moment the only sounds in the hallway were the bubbled, strangled breathing of the unconscious man at her feet.

And then Jordan reappeared, his shirt slightly twisted, face grim.

"That's taken care of." So matter-of-fact.

It was a good thing they were on the same team.

She reached out to straighten his T-shirt but stopped halfway there, her arms hanging out awkwardly. Maybe that wasn't okay. Maybe she wasn't allowed to just touch him whenever the thought popped into her head.

His brows drew close together as he stared at her hands.

Oh, forget it. This side of two hours ago, he'd had her pressed against a wall, kissing her silly. This wasn't anywhere close to that level.

Grabbing the cotton by the crooked seams, she gave it a little tug until the V of his collar pointed straight down, and the sides of the shirt lined up with the sides of his body.

"Oh." He smoothed out any remaining wrinkles with one of his hands—his other still holding the weapon. "Thanks."

"You're welcome." Because suddenly this had turned into tea on the veranda at Aunt Rosemarie's.

She should say something. Anything. Nothing could be worse than this uncomfortable silence, while one of her hands still rested on the hem of his shirt at his hip. His body was warm and alive, and a rush of gratitude set her skin on fire.

One or both of them could have been killed. Suddenly the two feet between them was too much, and she flung her arms around him, holding him tight, bumping into the pistol but not caring.

"I'm glad you're okay." Stupid. Stupid girl. She should have been able to come up with something smarter than that inane pronouncement, but the words had vanished, replaced only by the momentary need for a physical connection.

"Me?" His chuckle rumbled deep in his chest beneath her hear. "You're the one who risked everything."

"I know. It was a terrible idea."

"It's never a terrible idea if it works." His hand made a lazy circle on her back, and she shivered beneath his touch. Probably still the adrenaline leaving her system.

Sure, that seemed valid.

It couldn't possibly be that she really only wanted him to hold her. Which he did as if he'd been training for it his whole life. His steely arms were somehow both gentle and strong, and when she leaned against him, she had no doubt that he could keep her standing, no matter what.

His heart beat steadily under her ear, and she closed her eyes to the steady rhythm.

"I was a little bit scared." Her confession came out more easily than she'd imagined.

She'd always felt that she had to be so strong with him. Especially after their failed date, she couldn't show him her weaknesses or risk being vulnerable. Again.

So she'd put up her walls and kept him at bay. Staying angry with him, that was the easy part. It kept her safe. Protected. It meant she'd never risk another heartbreak.

And, oh, she'd been heartbroken. She'd never told a soul, but she'd been halfway in love with Jordan for nearly half her life.

She wasn't alone, of course. All of Neesha's friends had fallen in love with him at some point. But the rest of them had moved on.

Amy had been stuck.

Hoping. Wishing. Praying that one day he might notice her. One day he might realize that she was more than little-cousin material. One day he might prove to her that everything she'd learned about men from her father was wrong.

Only he hadn't.

He'd confirmed it all.

Starting with Neesha's engagement party.

Flames shot up her cheeks at the mere memory of that disaster, and she tried to pull away from his embrace. But the steel of his arms held strong.

"What's going on in that mind of yours?"

"Nothing."

"Liar." It was half teasing, half accusation. "We're not done, you know? But before we go through that door, I need to know that your focus is in the right spot." He took a deep breath, and her head moved with his chest. "You want to tell me what you're thinking about?"

She pinched up her face to keep anything in her expression from giving her away, wishing it was enough to make her disappear. "Not really."

"Too bad." How did he get his voice to be so authoritarian? There was absolutely zero room for negotiation or argument. And somehow she knew that if she lied to him, he'd know that, too.

"I was thinking about why this is so much easier than Neesha's engagement party."

"You mean, when you threw your entire plate of spareribs and collard greens in my lap?"

"Yes."

Every muscle in her body tensed, and so did his. How would he reply? With an excuse? An apology? Another false promise to placate her?

"I deserved it," he said.

She'd have fallen to the floor in that minute if he hadn't been holding her. "What?"

"I was a jerk. I didn't mean to be, but I was... Listen, I'd been getting a lot of pressure from my family to settle down, make grandbabies, carry on the family name. You know how that is."

Yes. She'd heard the teasing. She knew Aunt Phyllis and Aunt Ruth and Uncle Bobby weren't going to let up on him until he brought a girl home. Permanently.

Was it so terrible that once upon a time she'd hoped it would be her?

"When I showed up with you at the party, it was like walking into a firefight only to discover I'd forgotten my gun and worn an orange vest." The metal in his voice began to soften, regret lacing the words. "I tried to explain to them that I hadn't brought you as my date— that it was just easier for us to come together. We were on the same flight. It made sense to only get one rental car. Why waste the money?"

"But they didn't want to hear it."

He nodded his chin into her hair. "And when they started teasing you and me and asking when our engagement party would be, I needed to shut it down."

"Why?"

Oh, dear Lord, why did I say that? I don't want to know. I don't want to know. I don't want to know.

"They all love that I'm a SEAL, that I'm serving my country. But they don't get that it means that I don't know if I'm coming home."

He was so matter-of-fact about it that she jerked away. She must have surprised him because he dropped his arms, and she stepped back.

With his hands now free, he put one on his hip and the other at the back of his neck. "When I said that I'd never date you, it wasn't about… It didn't have anything to do with…" He let out a frustrated sigh. "You're amazing, right? You know that?"

Her stupid eyes started burning the second his voice dropped like that, and she clamped them shut, praying they wouldn't leak or give away how vulnerable she felt at the moment.

She could be hard and tough and play with the boys at work, but at the end of the day, she was still a woman. With all the unruly emotions that came with it.

"I just…I'm not in a place to be…I can't settle down right now. With anyone. I can't make promises about a life and a future together that I don't know if I can keep." And then, as if that wasn't a strong enough dismissal, he added, "But whoever you choose, he's going to be a really fortunate guy."

"Sure." Because what other insipid response could she give?

When she finally risked opening her eyes, he was staring at her, hard. "I'm sorry I hurt you."

"Sure."

"Okay." He leaned in to her side, and she shifted to return a quick hug.

Only it wasn't a hug. It was a kiss on the cheek. Except when she moved, it wasn't just on the cheek.

His lips caught the corner of her mouth, and they both froze. Because, for at least a moment, no one was chasing them. They weren't hiding from anyone. No one was going to interrupt them.

And his lips were on hers.

His eyes flashed wide-open, but he didn't pull away.

Her heart skipped a beat, maybe two, and all the air on the ship seemed to vanish.

And in a flash she was back in his arms, his lips fully pressed against hers, his arms snaking around her back.

She bumped into the submachine gun hanging from his shoulder, and he mumbled against her lips. "Safety's on."

Good, she thought. But she couldn't be bothered to respond aloud. There were more pressing things at hand. Like getting lost in his embrace. Like realizing that she'd never felt quite so cherished before in her entire life. Like knowing that no other man in the world could live up to this.

She rested her hands on his shoulders, then

the back of his neck, her thumb doing a lazy dance against his nape. He shivered, and a low groan in the back of his throat draped over them.

He wasn't distracted the way he had been the last time—watching for their pursuers. And the difference in his kiss was black-and-white versus Technicolor.

Even with her eyes closed, she knew that everything was brighter, louder, sweeter in Jordan Somerton's arms. She wiggled closer, holding him tighter, wishing this never had to end.

One of his hands slid into her hair, and he tilted her head to the side, increasing their connection.

She forgot her own name.

Her body felt like she'd been dipped in seltzer water. Everything tingled from the top of her head to the tips of her toes.

Oxygen had become a secondary need to being this close and this connected to him. Even when her lungs began to complain, she didn't pull away.

Finally, it was Jordan who broke the kiss. Gasping for air, he pressed his forehead to hers. "I'm sorry. I haven't done that in a while."

"You mean since this morning."

"No." His head rocked against hers, and his fingers curled into her waist. "I mean, kiss someone because I wanted to." He grasped for another breath. "Not because I had to."

"Oh." She shouldn't be surprised. Obviously he'd wanted to kiss her. She'd just assumed that handsome SEALs had their pick of the girls.

Apparently he was serious about what he'd said before. He believed he couldn't be in a relationship, couldn't be both a SEAL and a boyfriend.

Clearly he hadn't been paying attention to the five guys on his team, who had had no trouble realizing their lives were a million times richer because of the women who loved them. Matt, Tristan, Will, Luke and even Jordan's best friend, Zach. They'd figured out that life was too short to ignore love.

Not that she loved him.

She did not.

What she'd felt as a girl was infatuation. What she'd dreamed of as a young woman was a fairy tale. What she knew now was true.

If he wasn't interested—in it with his whole heart—then he'd wind up just like her dad.

And she'd had enough broken hearts to last a lifetime.

Keeping up the wall was easier. Hanging on to the memories of the times she'd been hurt didn't feel great. But it was better than fresh pain.

"It's okay. We'll just forget it happened." Or remember that it happened and have dreams about it but never speak of it again. Ever.

That was probably more realistic.

Cupping her elbows, he squeezed her carefully. "I'm sorry, Amy. I shouldn't have let myself get so carried away."

"Didn't you hear me? I said it's okay."

"That doesn't mean you don't deserve an apology."

There were no words to follow that. She'd had a lot of experience letting guys off the hook, but this was a first. She'd given him an out, and he wasn't taking it.

"Oh, man!"

The sharp cry made her jump back, and Jordan dropped his hands as they both turned toward the person intruding on their private moment. Bo turned his head as his neck and cheeks went red. "Man, I didn't mean to—"

His words cut off as his gaze landed on the figure at their feet. A pool of blood had collected near the thug's head, and Bo's mouth dropped open. "Is he dead?"

"No. I just broke his nose."

"Like, you broke it. For real?"

Jordan looked at the kid, who was gazing

up at him like he was a superhero come to life. "Only way I know how."

Amy bit back a snort, and Jordan winked at her, his lips fighting a grin.

"I saw you take out the other guy."

Her head whipped up. "What?"

"On the monitor. I was tracking you to see where you'd go." Bo ducked his head, almost in embarrassment. "Man, I've never seen anyone do a choke hold like that."

That explained why there had been no gunshots. Jordan didn't need them to subdue a terrorist.

If she hadn't been watching him, she'd have missed Jordan's response, an easy shrug. "There a reason you came to find us?"

"I almost forgot." Bo shook his shoulders and leaned in close, like he was about to reveal state secrets. "Staff Captain Xavier came into the security office. He was whispering with Second Officer Garfield. I don't think anyone was supposed to overhear, but I did. And I thought you'd want to know."

Jordan nodded but had to prompt Bo to continue. "Know what?"

"Radar picked up another boat coming in port side. It's headed our direction, and it ain't another cruise liner, neither."

"Is there any chance it's Coast Guard?" Jordan caught her gaze.

A tiny bubble of hope sprang to life. *Please. Please.*

"No. It's not official, and it's not announcing itself or responding to our hails."

Amy's heart took a nosedive to her toes. Her head spun, and she stumbled when the ship hit an unexpected swell.

Jordan grabbed her elbow but didn't address her unsteadiness. "Sounds like someone is *arriving.*"

They were on the same page. He remembered it, too. Eric Dean had mentioned it early on. They had to have Elaina when "they arrived." Apparently *they* were almost here.

But a ship didn't only mean an arrival. It could mean a departure.

Elaina's.

Though her mouth was painfully dry, she forced herself to speak. "We've got to find her. Right now."

Jordan didn't even reply. He simply turned to Bo and said, "You want to be part of our mission?"

"Seriously?" His fair eyebrows rose high. "What do you want me to do?"

"I need a rifle. A good one, preferably with a scope."

His face fell. "But all the weapons are locked up to keep them out of the passengers' hands. So we don't end up with one of those situations where the prisoners take over the prison. You know, like in the movies?"

Jordan waved his submachine gun in the air. "You mean like this?"

"Umm…sort of."

Jordan clapped a hand on the Bo's shoulder, nearly buckling the scrawny young man. "Listen, there's a little girl in danger. And you can either be a hero or you can get out of the way. It's up to you."

Bo had clearly never been called out by a SEAL before, and he scrambled for a response. "No, sir. Yes. I mean, I can—" His head ticked to the side and his barely there whiskers shimmered in the light. "I might—"

"Good man. Meet me on the lido deck in twenty minutes."

Bo took off running, and Amy stared after him. "You think he's going to find you a rifle?"

"Would you say no to me?"

She shot him her fiercest scowl. "Right now?"

His chuckle was throaty and it wrapped around her. "Right now we're going to find Elaina."

TWELVE

Hollywood always made the terrorist's lair dark and foreboding, but the stairwell, which had until recently been guarded by two burly men with minimal skill, was rather well lit.

Jordan held the Uzi at the ready as he ran down the steps, Amy close at his six.

He was missing his flack jacket, SIG Sauer and the seven-inch blade generally tucked into his boot.

But at least he had a weapon in his hand.

As they eased into the passageway, he scanned it for any activity. There was a small commotion at the mouth of the kitchen—someone had fired up the grill a little too high, and flames licked at the white dishes on the upper shelves. A short man was yelling at two others.

Other than that, there was only one man in their vicinity. He sat on the floor, his chin resting on his chest and hands folded over the white jacket covering his stomach. Definitely not a watchman.

But something was off. He could practically smell it.

"Where is everyone?" Amy whispered.

The other kitchen entrance had been hopping, housekeeping and waiters and other staff on assignment.

It almost felt as though someone had ordered this side to be kept clear.

Suddenly a scream ripped the air into shreds.

The three men at the grill looked up then quickly down, their argument forgotten. But no one moved to investigate the sound.

Amy's eyes grew round, her lips nearly disappearing into a line. "That was Elaina."

"You sure?"

"I heard her scream right before I blacked out." There wasn't an inch of give in her voice. "I'm sure."

It had come from somewhere at the far end of the hall, so he nodded that way. They crept along the bulkhead, silent and always at the ready for whatever they might face.

He checked each door as they passed it. First he pressed his ear to the frame, then he turned the handle. But each one was silent. No commotion. No more screams.

And the ones that opened showed only storage closets.

When he opened a door halfway down the hall, revealing a room with shelves full of cleaning supplies, Amy took a sharp breath. "I was in here. This is where I escaped." Her eyes darted from the tiny cubicle down the hall and back. "I was so close to Elaina."

The regret in her words nearly sliced him open, but he couldn't let it freeze them in place. They had to keep moving forward.

Suddenly another scream echoed through the walls.

And it was followed quickly by the footsteps of four very large men. They were still a good fifteen yards away, and if their raised voices were any indication, they hadn't noticed that they were being observed.

"Shut her up." That American accent and blond hair couldn't be missed. Stein was still in the picture. And he was speaking to Eric Dean, who held a writhing Elaina in his arms.

"I told you to keep it down," Dean hissed at the girl.

Amy leaped for them, but Jordan pulled her into the closet.

"What are you doing?" The words barely made it out from between her clenched teeth as she struggled against his hold. "They're moving her, and we both know if they get her off this boat, I'm never going to see her again." There was no emotion now. She'd put it away and put on her work mask. "We have to go for her now or we'll lose our chance. Don't you see that?"

"I hear you, but charging them directly right now is not what's best for her, and you know it. What would you have me do, spray this gun into that group of men—one of whom is holding Elaina? Take them out one by one, giving them time to kill her between shots if I didn't accidentally hit her myself?"

Amy's face turned ashen, and the gun in her hand shook.

And all of a sudden he realized that he wasn't only talking to a DEA agent, his partner on this mission. He was talking to a desperate aunt who had had her niece stolen right out from under her.

"I'm sor—" he tried to say, but she cut him off.

"You're right." She jerked her shoulders back, looking in the direction that Elaina had been taken. "But I'm not going to let them get away."

"Me, neither."

"All right, so what's your grand plan?"

He scrubbed at his face, buying just a fraction of a minute to put the pieces together. "She can't be transferred to the other boat unless it's moored to this ship, right? And if they're looking for any kind of fast getaway, they're not going to use chains. Probably ropes. And ropes can be cut. In order to keep her on this ship, we have to make sure they can't get to the other boat."

He could read the annoyance in her eyes. She was ready to go in, guns blazing, but he had a plan that might actually work, even if it wasn't the tactic she'd prefer.

"You going to shoot the ropes out?"

"I'm sure going to try."

"And if Bo doesn't come through with a rifle?"

He pushed a lock of her hair out of her face. "Then we go to your plan. Blazing guns and all that."

She sucked on her front tooth for a long second. "We going to split up?"

He knew she was still focused on tactics, but there was something in the words that made his heart ache, like it might be the end of what they'd shared.

It had to be, but that didn't mean he particularly wanted it to be that way.

"I think it makes sense. I need the high ground to get the right angle to take my shot."

Which was right where Bo was supposed to meet him.

"You okay following her from a distance?" Jordan continued. "Stein is in that group. If he sees you, he's not going to let you get away again."

Oof. Those words even hit him hard.

This was a bad idea. A very bad one. They should stick together. They should wait for backup. They should do anything but split up while hoping for the best.

But hoping for the best wouldn't get the job done. There was no backup coming, no one for them to rely on but each other.

He wasn't sending a novice out to do a job. She was highly trained and fully capable. And now she was armed.

The impressive 45mm Glock looked good in her hands, a reminder that she'd been trained and certified and was entirely competent. Not to mention strong. Determined. Dedicated. Beautiful.

And she was—the most beautiful woman he'd ever seen. All that soft-as-silk hair curling around her shoulders and those deep, expressive eyes that couldn't hide anything. Not that they ever tried to.

He'd been an absolute idiot not to beg her for a second chance on their sort-of date the minute he'd returned from Lybania.

But then where would he be? Right where

he was now. Able to offer her a couple of sweet kisses and friendship and not a single thing more.

She deserved better than that. And he knew it.

And none of it changed the fact that he was going to send her out after a man who wanted to see her dead.

Yep. This was a terrible idea.

"All right. I'm going to follow them. And if I get any chance to snatch Elaina, I'm going to take it." Her eyes sparked with fire, like she'd been working toward this her entire life. "When you snap the mooring ropes, what's your next move?"

"Truthfully? I haven't figured that part out yet."

Amy took off after Elaina, a prayer on the tip of her tongue and the top of her mind.

God, please keep Elaina safe. And me. And Jordan, too.

It had probably been years since she'd prayed for him. But somehow, in less than twenty-four hours, he'd woven his way back into her life and her mind in a very real way.

And even though they'd never be more than what they had been, she needed to know that he was out there, putting his very life on the line to save the innocents.

Pushing thoughts of Jordan out of her mind, she focused on the pursuit of her niece's captors. She had to somehow keep up with them but not get close enough for them to see her.

Her footsteps stayed silent as she listened for any sign of them.

Extra voices wove in and out of the service hallway, and she held her breath, pausing for just a moment.

Suddenly a man and a woman turned the corner in front of her, walking toward her direction.

She shoved her gun behind her back and held her breath as they approached. She hadn't seen either before, and they sure didn't look like they belonged with the terrorists. But she couldn't assume anything.

The gun in her hand was solid, and she held it with a firm—but not too firm—grip.

As they approached, the couple looked at her for only a brief moment. She gave them a curt nod and a half smile, and they passed without a word.

She let out her breath in a slow sigh and hurried along in the direction she'd been going. But even that short pause might have been too long. The men were no longer in sight. Had she lost Elaina again?

Heart thumping and ears ringing, she picked up her speed.

She had to find her niece.

But the hallway ahead was empty. And the blue carpet showed only normal wear patterns—no clear indicators of recent footsteps.

She turned around and raced toward another offshoot of the main hall. Maybe they'd gone that direction?

But it was empty, too.

Oh, Lord, where did they go?

She could barely hear her own thoughts over the thunder in her mind. They had to be here. They couldn't have disappeared so quickly. But if she chased down another hallway and it was the wrong choice, she'd lose them for good.

She slammed to a stop against a wall where two passageways merged into one, resting at the base of the Y and praying for all she was worth.

"Come on, Elaina. Tell me where you are."

The scream was high and loud and sweet music to her ears. There was no denying that it came from the left fork, and she chased its echo. Her feet were moving so fast that she nearly missed an offshoot and was halfway across its opening before she realized that it led to the service elevators, where a band of men and a writhing little girl waited.

Amy flung herself back against the wall, praying that Elaina's fuss had distracted them enough that no one realized they weren't alone.

She held her breath to keep from taking ragged breaths, hope filling a balloon in her chest and then popping it before it could be fully realized.

Elaina was right there. And Amy had six bullets in her gun. More than enough to take out the four men. But Jordan's words filled her, reminding her.

She might get off one or two shots, but not before someone took out Elaina. If she could just remain patient—patient and vigilant—she could get her back.

Amy closed her eyes and waited for the next movement. A fraction of a second later, the elevator doors groaned as they opened. Heavy footfalls trampled onto the metal floor, and the doors squeaked closed again.

She waited just long enough to make sure the doors were all the way closed before rushing around the corner. Just as she'd hoped, there was a set of adjacent stairs.

It was a race.

She took the steps two at a time, her running shoes landing as softly as she could upon the metal. Sometimes they clanged loudly and she cringed. But she didn't stop. Not even when she passed a group of housekeepers in their gray uniforms. They were moving much slower than she was, and one of them grumbled as she pushed past. "What's she doing here in such a hurry?"

"She's fit," said one of her coworkers. "Probably exercising."

If only her physical fitness was all that was at stake. Amy pressed on, deck after deck. At each level she pressed her ear against the wall, listening for the sound of the elevator. As long as it kept moving, so did she.

Her legs were trembling after five decks, her heart hammering so hard she was sure the sunbathers two decks below could hear it. When she flattened herself against the wall and listened, there was only the thump-thump of her own pulse and the rasp of her jagged breath.

Holding her breath and willing her heart to slow down, she waited.

Nothing.

The elevator had stopped. This was her floor.

Leaning back to tell Jordan, she stopped herself short and shook off the feeling of being all alone, abandoned.

God, why do I always jump there?

She stared up toward the heavens and waited for an answer. It wasn't too much to ask, was it? She'd had success in her career. She'd found a way to make a difference in the world. She was respected and had been honored on more than one occasion. So why did her mind insist on reminding her every chance it got of all the times that she'd been ignored, forgotten and left behind?

Jordan hadn't left her behind this time. They'd mutually agreed that by splitting up they could cover more ground. He was off doing his part of the job. And she was doing hers.

And it meant that she'd have to wait to listen for answers.

Poking her head out of the stairwell, she made a quick survey of the situation. The elevator doors were closed, and the niche was empty, save for two service carts lining the far wall.

She raced toward the metal carts, ducking between them and out of sight just as the telltale groan of the elevator doors began. She pulled a loose bedsheet over her, maintaining only a partial view.

"Hurry up." She'd recognize Stein's voice anywhere at this point, and he spat out orders to the other three men. "They're pulling the boat in now. It can't stay docked for long. And she has to be on it when it pulls away. The general won't accept any less."

General? But Abkar was awaiting trial in a US prison. Was he pulling strings from behind bars?

Where was Jordan when she needed to talk this through with him?

Don't dwell on that, Delgado.

The entourage turned left, and she slipped after them, thankful for the silence of padded carpet compared to the clanging metal stairs she'd left behind. They went halfway down the hall and then entered a cabin—one of the most expensive on board with a semiprivate deck overlooking the port side of the ship.

Right where the unnamed boat was to meet up with the cruise ship.

Her stomach sank as sure as an anchor at sea.

This was all going down on the outer deck, but she was stuck inside. She had to figure out a way to get through one of these rooms. The outer decks on this part of the boat were each separated by a partial wall, and if she could just get to one, she could work her way down the row.

It was the getting through the room that would take some effort. She needed Jordan to kick the door in. But she didn't have Jordan.

She needed help. An idea. Anything.

She twisted and spun, looking for something that would help.

And then, like a gift, a squeaking wheel rolled in her direction. She looked up just as a maid pushed one of the service carts in her direction. She was busy counting towels, and Amy jumped into the notch of a door to get out of her way. Holding her breath, she waited for the cart to stop, which it finally did. At the far end of the hall, just three doors down from the one Elaina had disappeared into.

Thank You. Thank You.

It was the only prayer that she could complete as she flew toward the cart. The maid had propped the door open as she pulled out soiled towels and sheets, and Amy didn't think twice before racing through.

"Hey. Hey, what are you doing?"

Amy didn't even pause, flinging open the sliding glass door to the private balcony. The sun was bright to eyes that had spent so much time inside the bowels of the ship, and she blinked against the white spots that flashed before her, rushing toward the partial wall that separated her from the neighboring deck.

But before she could launch herself over, the thrumming sound of a second boat reached her ears, and she looked over the railing and down at what looked like a midsize fishing boat.

She couldn't imagine the fishing boat managing the open ocean for very long—it simply didn't have the fuel capacity for long journeys— but no matter how hard she looked, she couldn't see land in any direction.

Where it had come from wasn't nearly as important as who was about to be on it, and where they were going, so she grabbed the top of the first wall and pulled herself up.

The partial wall was at least six feet tall—offering relative privacy to each of the cabins. Scrambling over it wasn't quite as easy as she'd hoped.

The last time she'd scaled a wall, it had been made of wood and boasted a knotted rope. This one was mostly metal, its panels slippery against the toes of her shoes. But she worked her legs up and up until she was on top of the wall and then slid to the floor on the other side.

It was empty save a table and two chairs, and she gave a quick peek into the room on the other side of the glass door to make sure that it was empty, too. No need to have a surprised observer as she scaled the next wall.

The second wall took a little longer than the first, her fingers and arms aching with the strain.

She hadn't used these muscles in a long time, and by the time she was on the other side of the wall from Elaina, every single inch of her trembled.

Moderating her breathing, she pressed against the barrier and peeked over the edge of the ship. The fishing boat below bobbed a few dozen yards away. And even though she'd climbed five decks, it wasn't terribly far below them. Too far to jump, but with a ladder…

And then she realized that the ship was already secured to the cruise liner. Ropes thicker than her forearms swung between the two vessels, bobbing and dipping out of the water.

Plenty of time had passed since Bo had told them security was aware of the approaching boat. Where was security now? Why wasn't the captain doing something?

She looked around frantically for help but was still alone. The crew seemed to be on vacation. Or was somehow tied to this conspiracy. Because if anyone was paying attention, there was no way they'd have let this happen unless they were in on it.

She was alone.

You're not alone. You have Jordan.

The ship rocked on a large wave. The ropes pulled tight but held. And Amy thought she might be sick. She'd expected that the arrival meant someone would be boarding the ship, but now it was clear from this angle that the boat's only goal was taking someone away. Taking Elaina away.

Okay, Jordan. Where are you? We need you.

The sliding door on the other side of the wall rolled open, and angry voices started shouting.

"There it is."

Amy peeked around the edge of the barrier, and her eye almost missed a metal wire running from the balcony straight to the boat. It didn't seem to be holding the boat secure, and there was a little slack in the line. It quivered as if someone on the other side strummed it.

"Looks stable. You ready to go?"

"Yep. My harness is good."

"Okay, put her in the vest." That was Stein. "Get her attached to the line."

It wasn't just any line. This was a zip line. Forget the ladder—they were going to slide Elaina right into the hands of someone on that boat.

No. No. No. This could not be happening.

"No. Stop!" Elaina's voice was strong and demanding, and Amy had never been so proud to be her aunt.

"Shut up!" The sickening smack of a hand on flesh made Amy recoil and Elaina wailed. "You better keep your mouth shut, or you're never going to make it to that other boat. You understand?"

Whatever Elaina was being threatened with— a gun? a knife?—made her scream, and Amy had to physically hold herself back from crashing through the wall. Pistol in hand, she laid out all of her options.

Shoot into the unseen and pray she didn't hit Elaina.

Shoot over the water to distract them but alert them to her presence.

Scale the wall and try to tackle at least two, maybe four men, risking injury and the inability to fight back.

These weren't options. They were ludicrous.

She couldn't do this alone.

God, I need help!

THIRTEEN

Jordan burst into the sunlight, its brilliance nearly blinding him, and he held up his arm while his eyes adjusted. The vacationers who had packed onto the lido deck were oblivious to the boat off the port side, but it was nearly all he could see. The small vessel held the telltale cranes and nets of a fishing boat, but it was capturing a different type of fish today.

Zigzagging between deck chairs and towels spread across the ground, he chose a place along the rail and took stock of the ropes strung between the ships.

The new arrival wasn't close enough to the cruise liner to make for an easy transfer. But it was obvious that the plan was to get Elaina away from the ship. So why was it so far way?

Or, better yet, why not use a vessel that could pull closer to the ship?

He turned to Amy to see what she thought.

Then he remembered that he was on his own. At least for now.

Amy would be back. For sure.

For now, he had to break the ties that bound the two boats together. Said ties were made of four-inch-thick rope and loose enough to lose any benefit from tension, which was a problem. The tighter the rope, the easier it would snap when broken. Loose rope could be damaged without breaking.

He needed those ties to pull taut. And he needed a rifle.

Pulling away from the rail, he made a quick survey of the area. No sign of Bo.

Had he misjudged the young man? The kid had seemed so eager for a pat on the back and the hope that someday he might become one of the elite. Surely he wouldn't let his new hero down…would he?

Jordan had never taken advantage of his place on the teams, but he knew there were those who would do anything to get in good with a SEAL. And it was generally the young ones who wanted a trident pin of their own.

So, where was he?

"Mr. Somerton." It was barely a panted breath, but Jordan turned with a smile on his face to see Bo racing toward him, a rifle held out at arm's length. Several women screamed and jumped to their feet, but Bo paid them no mind.

The kid had a lot to learn to earn the title of SEAL, but at the moment, Jordan had never seen anything better.

"Good man." He clapped Bo on the back, accepting the weapon and weighing it in his hand. It wasn't quite right. It wasn't his. But it would do in a pinch.

"That man has a gun!" a mom screamed and frantically collected her children. "Get inside, now!"

Bo looked over his shoulder, his eyes round. "I guess maybe I shouldn't have held it out like that."

"Maybe not. But we don't have any time to lose. That ship, it's here."

"I know." Bo's voice took on an urgent whisper. "Everyone in the security office is going crazy. Made it easy to take off with the rifle, but Staff Captain Xavier has been yelling at the guys—even the ones off shift—to line the lower decks and keep anyone unauthorized from boarding this ship. And no one can find the captain."

His heart gave a hard thump. "The captain's missing?"

"Yep. No one's seen him in, like, three hours."

"Who's running the ship, then?"

"Staff captain."

This didn't line up. The captain disappearing when the other boat was meeting up with them was a coincidence he couldn't ignore. Either the captain was in on this whole thing—which would explain Eric Dean's escape—or he'd been taken out of commission.

Jordan hoped it was the later—and only temporarily. No captain would willingly give up his command. An image of the incapacitated officer flashed across his mind and made his skin crawl.

Whatever had happened, if the captain had been taken out of commission then someone else had control of the ship. And Xavier might not even realize it.

Until he knew what exactly was going down on the bridge, Jordan couldn't trust anyone. Except Amy.

And maybe Bo.

"Did you bring me any rounds?"

Bo's face broke into a broad smile. "Course I did." He reached into his pocket and pulled out a handful of ammo.

Jordan scooped the bullets up and shoved them into his pocket.

"Bo, I need you to do me a favor."

"Anything."

Jordan nearly smiled at the young man, so

eager he was almost dancing on his toes. "Get this ship moving hard starboard."

"Excuse me?"

"We need to move to the right. Right now."

"But…" Bo pointed toward the bridge, his finger rolling in the air. "That's up to the senior officers. We've got to stay on course and everything."

Jordan clapped his hand on Bo's shoulder firmly, forcing him to understand. "We won't get off course. We only need to shift direction for a minute, but this has to happen. Right now. And you're the only man for the job."

"But what do I say?"

"Tell them a little girl's life is on the line. Tell them you saw her on the monitor. Tell them they're going to save her right now. Just steer starboard."

Bo's face went slack, but he quickly recovered. "Okay. I'll do it." He bolted away, and Jordan prayed the boy would find a way to get the job done.

In the meantime, he had his own job to do.

As he lifted the rifle to his shoulder, a rush of rightness flowed through him. This is what he knew. This is what he did.

But a bloodcurdling scream from across the lido deck reminded him that not everyone felt that way about a weapon in his hands. He glanced over at the young woman yanking off her headphones and jumping to her feet, clearly only now realizing what the rest of the crowd had discovered minutes before. She held a towel in front of her like it might save her life. Her lips trembled, and she never blinked, her gaze always on him.

"Ma'am." He nodded in greeting, keeping his voice low. "You might want to head inside. This is going to be loud."

She jerked her chin up and down several times before dashing across the wooden slats. Halfway to the exit, she stopped, turned back to look at her bag, and then clearly made the choice to leave it behind as she kept running.

He leaned into the railing, watching the fishing boat through the scope and following the lines across the water.

Suddenly the sunlight glinted off something he hadn't seen before. It wasn't part of the boat or the rope. Maybe it was just the crest of a wave.

Nope. There it was again. He caught his breath and waited. Again.

The stock of the rifle dug into his shoulder as he leaned his elbows on the wooden rail.

Suddenly the light hit it just right, and he realized what he was looking at. It was a zip line.

He couldn't see exactly where it began, but it absolutely ended on the fishing boat.

If he'd had any hair on the back of his neck, it would have stood up on end.

They were going to slide Elaina off the ship. Most likely never to be seen again.

Unacceptable. Period.

The line was tight, which worked for him. What didn't work for him was his blind spot. From this angle there was no way to tell if anyone—such as Elaina—was on the line.

But every second he waited was another that she might be attached to that line and pushed off the ship.

Oh, Lord, let her not be on it now.

He checked his rifle once more, focused through the scope and lined up his shot.

Smooth is fast.

He took a deep breath, released it and eased his trigger finger back.

Crack.

The shot echoed and everyone on board knew someone was shooting now.

But the bullet veered left, missing its mark.

How could that be? He'd had it lined up perfectly.

His stomach sank. The scope was off. But there wasn't time to worry about that. He had to recalibrate and fire again.

He found his mark, adjusted for the errant scope and let out a prayer with his breath. Then he squeezed the trigger, and it was like the whole world exploded.

The wire snapped audibly, the sound of the recoil covering this side of the ship.

But his job wasn't done. Reloading his weapon, he took aim at the still-sluggish ropes. He got off round after round into the lines, fraying them but not succeeding in snapping them the way he wanted to. They were just too loose.

"Stop. Put your hands up now!"

Jordan paused but kept his weapon in place as two security guards approached. They both carried pistols, arms extended and elbows locked.

Oh, man. It was going to hurt when he took them out.

He almost felt bad. They weren't trained for this—for any of it. For pirates in the middle of the Caribbean Sea. For a SEAL sniper with a rifle. But feeling bad for them didn't mean Jordan would hesitate to put them down. There were lives on the line here. The safety of the ship and everyone on it—including his family— was at risk. And, most of all, Amy was counting on him. Jordan wasn't going to let anything stand in his way.

"Listen, guys. You can put your guns down. I'm not aiming at anyone."

The rounder one looked at his skinny friend and shook his head quickly. They continued their approach. "Just put it down, man."

Jordan let the rifle swing from the strap at his shoulder and held his hands up. "Take it easy." He stepped toward them slowly, evenly, maintaining eye contact the whole time. "It's okay. I don't want to hurt anyone."

Well, that was mostly true. He genuinely didn't want to hurt these guys—though he wouldn't be opposed to getting a few blows in on Stein. But with the guards, he wouldn't do any permanent damage. As long as they cooperated. If they tried to fight back—well, he just couldn't make any promises at that point.

The men responded well to his soothing tones and their weapons lowered as he drew within three feet.

That was their biggest mistake.

His arm swept down without warning, taking both of their firearms out in one motion. Guns clattered to the deck as one man fell to his knees after it, his forearm bent at an unnatural angle. He groaned, his face going white with pain as he reached for his weapon with the other hand. Jordan stepped on the guns, sliding them out of reach.

"I'm not going to hurt you guys." Well, not much more than he already had.

"Why are you doing this? What do you want?"

He narrowed his gaze onto them. "I'm trying to rescue a little girl."

"What girl?"

That was new. Shouldn't all the security personnel have been briefed? Surely Xavier had made certain that his team was looking for Elaina. He'd said he would do that, right?

Jordan tried to rack his brain, but suddenly the ship tipped starboard.

Way to go, Bo!

He raced for the railing just as the ropes pulled tight. They held for a long breath, and he pulled up his rifle again, just in case.

Snap. Pop.

The lines snapped and then broke apart.

The fishing boat rocked in the water, keeping up with the liner but now wholly disconnected.

"Gentlemen," he said, turning back to the injured guards. "You should probably get some medical attention." The guy with the broken arm looked about ready to pass out, and Jordan rotated his wrist in sympathy. His arm barely stung where he'd made contact. He should thank Lieutenant Sawyer for teaching him that move when he'd been fresh out of BUD/S.

Scooping up their pistols, he quickly checked them for other weapons. None.

Good. They couldn't do anything else to stop him from meeting up with Amy.

As long as she was where she said she'd be.

Amy nearly dropped to her knees at the first crack of a rifle, her pistol jumping into her hand.

But the shot wasn't aimed at her.

Soon after, a second echoed over the ship, and then the zip line tore in two, the sudden release of tension whipping it back and forth.

Her neighbors shouted in languages she'd never heard before, distracted and clearly blaming each other for a terrible plan.

This was it. Her chance.

It might be her only one.

Scaling the wall, she did a quick assessment from her position perched at the top. Eric Dean and another man argued with each other as Elaina stood crying before them. Two more rifle shots came in quick succession, and the men spun toward the sound, leaning over the railing. Stein had disappeared, but the sliding door to the room was open, the curtain waving in the wind.

Elaina looked up, her gaze locking on Amy, and her mouth opened.

Amy slammed a single finger in front of her lips.

With huge eyes rimmed in red, Elaina nodded.

Amy waved to the side as another rifle round shook the ship, and Elaina huddled in the corner.

Swinging over the wall, she landed in a squatting position. Before the men even realized she was there, she got off two knee shots, almost indistinguishable from the sounds of Jordan's rifle fire.

Both men screamed, dropping their weapons, which Amy scooped up and shoved into her pockets.

She wanted to hug her niece and bury her nose in Elaina's sweet hair and never let her go again, but there wasn't time for a proper reunion, so she scooped the girl into one arm and said, "Hold tight."

Elaina nodded, and Amy burst into the cabin.

Stein dropped his phone, his mouth hanging open as she flew through the door. It took him only a split second to grab for his gun, but it was too late.

She got off two rounds that hit his stomach with enough force to knock him on his back, sprawled across the bed. She didn't stop to check on him, to see if he was dead or to disarm him. There had been four men with Elaina, and she wasn't going to wait around to run into the last.

Rushing through the door, she raced for the

spot where she'd promised to meet Jordan—Michael's cabin.

The whole ship seemed to be in chaos, people screaming and cabin doors slamming. No one seemed to pay her or Elaina any mind. They were just another pair of people in a sea of confusion.

Amy didn't pay attention to the others, either—all of her focus was on Elaina's tears. She sobbed a great pool on Amy's neck, her hiccups shredding Amy's heart one piece at a time. Elaina's grip was unrelenting, digging into her neck like she would never let go.

"Honey, don't cry." The words were no better than a whisper, forced past the lump in her own throat. "You're safe now." Amy wrapped her other arm around Elaina's waist. Carrying her while running was awkward. Setting her down wasn't even an option.

"I was so-o scared."

Amy wished that she could wipe those memories away, praying they would be replaced with ones of joy and security, of flying high on park swings and hugging Michael.

"I'm going to take you to someplace safe, okay? This is all over. I promise."

But as she ran, she wondered if she could really make that promise with any hope of keeping it. Elaina wasn't in terrorist hands any longer, but manipulating Michael had been the goal all along, so their family was still in danger.

Without Elaina in their hands, what depths would the terrorists sink to?

She didn't have any idea how many more of them were on the ship or how long it would take before someone on the outside noticed that their ship was in distress.

Her stomach sank as she approached Michael's cabin. The door was closed, the hallway strangely silent. She set Elaina down and pressed her ear to the wood, praying Jordan was in there. He had to have made it back.

He'd done his part. The zip line had snapped, and it had been enough to keep the terrorists from sending her niece to the other boat. Elaina was free. But had he been caught?

"Daddy!" Elaina shrieked when Michael poked his head out of the doorway.

Michael scooped her into his arms, holding her and crying like he'd never stop. "Baby girl. I was so scared."

"Not out here." That voice brought every nerve ending in Amy's body to life. Jordan appeared like he'd always been there, and he ushered them into the suite, closing the door behind all of them. Michael sat Elaina on the edge of the couch and knelt before her, running his hands over her limbs and whispering over and over how much he loved her.

And suddenly, Amy couldn't keep from crying. A daddy who loved his daughter. A daughter who held on like he was her newest, best and only toy.

She knuckled away the tears rolling down her cheeks and refused to look anywhere remotely in Jordan's direction.

"I feel like we're intruding on a private moment. Maybe we should give them a minute."

She nodded, and they ducked outside, sharing the tiny niche removed from the hallway. She stared at the deck. He at the ceiling.

All she really wanted to do was ask him to hold her. Not in a wild kiss or strategic play. She just wanted him to put his arms around her and whisper that it was all going to be all right now. That everything was okay and they were safe. And that he wasn't going to leave her alone.

And that he loved her, too.

Oh, dear.

That was beyond inconvenient.

She didn't love him. She couldn't.

He'd made promises only to break them. This was not the man she could love.

Yet a tiny voice in her head that sounded too much like Neesha insisted that he was a good man and that she could trust him with her heart.

Except, she didn't trust *any* man with her heart.

At some point during her mental meanderings, his gaze had drifted to her, and she jumped to attention, certain he could see all of what she was feeling written across her face. So she blurted out the only thing she could think of. "Where'd you get the rifle?"

A slow smile sneaked across his lips. "Bo came through." Then he told her the whole story of Bo and the security guards and the ship with no captain. "I'm glad that Elaina's safe, but I can't help but feel like we're not done. Pirates are still hidden on this ship."

She knew the feeling. It felt like a brick was sitting in the bottom of her stomach. "And if they can't get Michael to comply through Elaina, they're going to try something else. Aren't they?"

His eyebrows dipped together, but he didn't have time to answer before a loud voice with a heavy accent came through the speaker system.

"Ambassador Michael Torres. You have twenty minutes to report to the bridge. If you—and all of your bodyguards—do not arrive, we will shoot one passenger every five minutes."

Amy's mouth went dry and her palms began to sweat.

"And we will begin with this one."

From farther away from the microphone, but

no less clear, came a voice she'd recognize anywhere. "Take your hands off me."

That brick in her stomach tripled in size, pushing all the air from her lungs and every thought from her brain, save one.

Neesha.

FOURTEEN

Jordan grabbed Amy's arm as she dashed down the hallway.

"Let me handle this." He tried to keep his voice steady, but there were too many pictures flooding his mind. Of Neesha being pulled from her suite, kicking and screaming, a gun to her head. Of Rodney being taken with her. Of the fear on her face and terror in her eyes. Of the smack she'd inevitably have taken across the cheek when she talked back to them.

And she would have. Because she was Neesha, and she was fearless.

And above all of those was one more image—of Amy at the mercy of these madmen.

Just the thought of it hit harder than a kidney shot, even as he tried to shake it off, to pretend that he hadn't felt the fear of losing her.

Because maybe the only thing worse than leaving someone behind was having them leave you.

That kind of pain was unacceptable. He'd

spent his entire life making sure that he'd never feel that way again—the way he'd felt when his dad hadn't come home. And he wasn't about to change his mind for a pretty smile with a fierce heart.

"I can't let you go."

She laughed in his face, but there was no humor to it. "It's not your choice."

He waved a hand at the closed door. "Someone needs to stay with Michael. Keep him from leaving this room."

Jerking her arm free from his grip, she leaned in until their faces were only inches apart. "That's my best friend up there."

"And she's my family. I'm better trained. I'm fully armed. And I'm not going to let you put yourself at risk. I need for—"

He slammed on the brakes. He'd been about to admit that he needed her to be safe and to be there and to never leave him. Because he'd never met anyone so maddeningly brilliant and tough. Because he cared about her.

Because he was head-over-heels, couldn't-wait-to-kiss-her-again, please-God-let-her-feel-the-same in love with her.

His head spun like he'd been clocked with a two-by-four.

No. Nope. Not going to happen.

Amy was the most vibrant, fierce woman he'd

ever met. But he could not, would not, be in love with her.

"Your family needs you to make it home. Elaina's already lost her mom. What would happen if she lost you, too?"

It was a low blow, and he saw the instant it landed.

Her mouth went slack, then closed, then opened again without a sound except the slow release of breath.

But he wasn't going to take it back. If she found it unforgiveable…then that was fine by him.

"Stay put. Keep them safe. Let me take care of this."

Eyes narrowing, she poked him in the chest with one finger. "And what about you? You don't think you have family waiting for you to come home? You don't think people care that you're safe?"

She jabbed him again in the same spot, and he backed up a step to rub at it.

Undeterred, Amy continued her rant. "You don't think that maybe some of us would want you to come home safely so we could have at least one more kiss?"

Wait. What?

"So we don't waste whatever time we might actually have together?" Her voice rose until it echoed around them. "So *some of us* can stop *daydreaming* about being in love and *actually* be in it?"

She slammed her mouth against his, grabbing his face between both hands and holding on until he couldn't breathe. It wasn't romantic or tender, but it nearly knocked his socks off. There was so much fire in her frame, and somehow he knew that one more kiss would never be enough between them. He'd always want another and another and another.

So he forced himself to pull back.

He couldn't make heads or tails out of anything she'd said, even without the kiss that jumbled it all together. All he knew was that seconds were ticking by until those madmen killed his cousin.

"No. No one wants that from me."

He had to believe that or he'd never be able to go. And he needed to.

He took off running without another word.

By Jordan's count there were eight guards surrounding the ship's bridge. None of them in uniform and all carrying Middle Eastern weapons. That was at least twice the number of Lybanians he'd counted on. And he couldn't see inside the bridge to tell how many more he'd face in there. But it didn't matter. Neesha was going to make it to her wedding day. Jordan would stand by Rodney and watch them commit to making a life together.

Someone deserved to be happy. Even if it wasn't an option for him.

But he pushed those thoughts away as he focused on what was ahead.

Each guard patrolled a small section of the bridge's perimeter alone.

Easy targets.

Jordan worked his way toward the guard nearest him. Sliding up behind him, Jordan wrapped an arm around his neck and jerked.

The man fell to the floor immediately, his eyes closed and chest rising with shallow gasps. He'd wake with a raging headache. But he wouldn't wake up anytime soon.

Jordan moved on to the next, who also went down without a fight.

But each confrontation took time, which he didn't have to spare.

Ten minutes had already slipped by and every minute that passed lowered the chance of being able to save Neesha.

It was too risky to charge the bridge without first taking out the men standing guard. But taking them out and tying them up one by one was too slow.

A knee shot would be more efficient. No

one walked away from a blown out knee, and it would certainly take them down long enough for him to take their weapons. Any shot would also alert whoever was running this ship that Michael wasn't coming. And then the innocents would start dying.

His stomach rolled, an image of Neesha lying in a pool of blood flashing across his mind's eye.

That wasn't an option. But he couldn't come up with any valid alternatives.

If only he could go back in time to three days before and tell his family never to get on this ship. If only they'd never left the port and everyone he loved was safe.

If onlys didn't get the job done.

Swinging his rifle to his shoulder, he took one step before a hand latched on to his shoulder.

He swung around, shoving his weapon into the face behind him.

"Amy?" But there was no real question to it. "What are you doing here?"

She pushed his gun out of her face with a hand that also held a fluffy red pillow. "I figured you could use some backup."

"But what about Michael and Elaina?"

She waved off his concern, a second pillow flouncing as she did so. "They're fine. They're safe. And they'll stay put with Pete. Besides, with everyone here watching for Michael, who's going to go after him?"

"Well—" She made a valid point. Rats.

"Besides, you can't take them all out moving this slow."

He jerked his head in the direction he'd been moving. "How long have you been following me?"

"Long enough." She shoved one of the pillows into his chest, and he had no choice but to take it from her. "Now, we have exactly seven minutes until this lunatic said he'd start shooting."

"And you want me to take a nap?"

She popped him upside the head with the other pillow. "Don't be a jerk. Take the pillow. Use it as a silencer. You take out a few kneecaps on that side. I'll take the other. And then we'll meet at the entrance to the bridge."

She sounded so sure about her plan that he nearly agreed without thinking. But he had an argument—a really good reason why she shouldn't be part of this operation. He was sure of it. He just wasn't entirely clear what it was at the moment.

No, watching Amy put herself in danger didn't work for him. But he'd tried telling her that. And it hadn't gone over well. And did he really have the right to hold her back? She was as trained and sure as any Marine he'd ever worked with. So why shouldn't he want her as a partner?

Because love didn't always make sense.

"Stop thinking, take the pillow and go." She looked at her watch. "We don't have time for whatever argument you're trying to make against this." With that, she dashed toward the far side of the deck, staying out of the line of sight from anywhere on the bridge.

Smart girl.

Smart woman.

Amazing woman.

"Shut up and go." He mumbled to himself as he took off in the opposite direction.

Amy aimed through her pillow and pulled the trigger halfway back. Ready to take her final shot. Well, at least her last one before they stormed the bridge. Already, her heart beat faster than it should, every thump heavy with anticipation.

All she had to do was get through this and meet up with Jordan. Then they'd free Neesha.

And then they'd call for help.

She let out a quick breath, preparing to take the shot.

Suddenly an arm wrapped around her throat

and jerked her of her feet. Her Glock clattered to the floor, the pillow falling right on top of it.

She gasped and clawed and tried to scream, but her windpipe was under attack, brutally constricted by a meaty forearm.

"You've done enough damage." Her attacker swore in her ear, calling her filthy names that made her skin crawl.

All the bruises from when she'd been choked to unconsciousness the night before throbbed even further under this abuse, but she refused to succumb.

Black curtains pulled across her peripheral vision, and she kicked down against his knee, pushing herself up to steal a breath. It was enough to pull back the veil for at least a moment, but it didn't dislodge his arm.

Hanging by her chin, feet kicking and fingers clawing for freedom, all the air in her lungs dwindled down to nothing. Her neck stretched, the weight of her body dragging her down.

She was going to miss Jordan. He'd be waiting for her, and she couldn't get to him. Funny how that was all that she could think about as her chest screamed for oxygen and her muscles trembled.

This time, she'd be the one standing him up. It wasn't because of another commitment or because she'd disappeared to someplace else she'd rather be. She just wasn't going to show.

Because sometimes there was no way around it.

Deep down, she'd known that all along. But she'd held on to a grudge because it was easier to be bitter than it was to admit just how raw her heart had been worn by a negligent father. And because keeping up that wall was so much easier than risking love.

Only it wasn't easier. It meant missing out on all the amazing things that God could have for her. It meant missing out on Jordan.

She cried out as loudly as her hoarse voice could manage. The sound didn't go far, but it elicited a growl in her ear.

"Shut up!" He slammed her into the wall, and she thought her body might just splinter.

This was it. She might not survive this attack.

She was never going to see that cocky grin when she finally told Jordan that she'd forgiven him. And she had. In that very moment.

She'd choose forgiveness every day of the week if it meant a chance to be with Jordan.

But she'd missed her chance. She was never going to see him or hold him. Or kiss him again.

And he'd think she hated him.

She didn't. Not even a little bit.

Her dad, either. All those years of anger and

resentment were useless. Such a waste of time and energy. She'd missed out on only God knew what kind of joy because she'd held on to hurts. The walls she'd thought protected her only robbed her.

Her dad hadn't changed.

Jordan couldn't be any more sorry than he already was.

She was the only one who had been hurt by refusing to release those memories.

What a waste.

But if she was going to meet her Maker today, she'd do it with a clear conscience.

God, forgive me for hating my dad for so long. Let him know somehow that I forgave him. Maybe he was doing his best. And no matter where he was, I was never alone. You were always with me. And be with Jordan, too. Protect him. Keep him safe. I'm so sorry that I held on to my anger when I should have shown him that I loved him.

The arm at her neck jerked again, and suddenly everything went black.

Jordan's flesh tingled as he slipped along the bulkhead below the bridge. His gaze darted across to the open deck and to the ladders leading to lower levels. All clear.

Except for that small voice in his head screaming that he'd missed something.

There was supposed to be one more guard. Where had the guy gone?

And where was Amy?

His stomach rolled, and something that could only be fear washed over him.

He didn't have time for fear on a mission. There was only focus and strategy and executing the plan. But this wasn't like any other mission. It had become something entirely different from the moment Amy had been taken the night before.

An uneasy sensation gnawed on his stomach with each step he took closer to the meet-up point. Despite the warmth of the sunshine and the blue sky, a black cloud hung low over him. He held his breath, his pistol at the ready.

Only he knew what he was going to find.

Nothing.

Just then the walkie-talkie he'd stolen from one of the guards he'd taken out squawked from the spot where he'd clipped it to his belt. "We got her," a sinister voice announced. "The DEA agent. Bringing her up right now."

Then he added, "She'll never make trouble for us again."

His heart stopped in that moment. It had no reason to keep beating. The one person he'd ever been in love with was about to lose her life. And he didn't have a plan, a backup or a hope in the world.

Jordan hid in the shadows below the bridge, waiting for any sign of Amy, counting down the seconds until whoever was calling the shots on this ship gave up waiting for Michael. As for what he'd do then…he honestly had no idea.

But he had to stay close if he was going to have any chance of protecting Neesha. And anyway, he wasn't going anywhere until he knew where Amy was.

"God, could You show up? Right now, please." His whisper was nearly inaudible as he stared toward the sky. He'd always trusted that he was heard when he prayed, but he'd still always done as much as he could in his own strength.

But now his own skill, experience and power weren't going to cut it.

Not even close.

I need You.

And then, as if God had only been waiting for him to come to that understanding, everything changed.

Two broad men strolled toward the bridge, arrogant and assured and thoroughly armed. And one of them carried Amy. Her body sagged, limp and pale.

His stomach rolled. Was she even alive?

He couldn't afford to ask himself questions like that. He could only believe that God had this covered. If he let himself dwell on the might-bes, he'd go crazy.

"Michael Torres. You have three minutes," the voice over the intercom singsonged as though he was enjoying taunting Michael, and Jordan spat next to his shoe. Terrorists liked to mock their victims. They thrived on perceived power and used psychological tricks to make their opponents feel helpless to stop them.

But it wasn't going to work.

Clearing his mind of everything but the scene before him, he played it out, visualizing every tactical maneuver. Stay low. Pie the corner—turning around a corner so he only revealed himself a step at a time while maximizing his view into the rest of the room.

He double-checked the rounds in his pistols and the rifle over his shoulder. Full magazines in each. One pistol in hand, one at the ready.

Time to go.

He ran for the entrance to the bridge and stopped just outside of the view of those inside, pressing his back to the wall.

"Get her up." The low growl sounded familiar, but Jordan couldn't quite place it. "We'll prove to the ambassador that we're serious."

Neesha screamed and Rodney yelled, but the sound of a fist against flesh quieted the room.

Perfect. Neesha, Rodney and Amy were all in there, all at risk of being caught by a stray bullet.

Jordan took a single step away from the wall, turning to face inside. Each small step revealed another slice of the room, so far showing him only empty computer consoles. The rest of the staff had either been run off or met the same fate as the captain, whatever that was.

On his fourth step, he spotted two figures. The one sprawled on the floor was clearly Amy. And the thug towering over her had to be a Lybanian, his dark hair hanging past his collar as he looked down his narrow nose at her.

"Time's up, Ambassador!"

The announcement came from both inside the bridge and the intercom above.

Before the speaker finished, Jordan said a quick prayer and fired his first shot. It hit the man's shoulder, and he stumbled backward, opening himself up to a second shot, this one to the throat.

He went down hard, just as the room erupted in shouts and gunfire.

No more hiding.

Jordan roared as he raced into the ship's control room, drawing as much attention as he could, taking a quick survey. Five men standing. The tango holding the microphone for the intercom also held a gun aimed at Neesha's head.

Pop. Pop. Pop.

He put three bullets into the man's chest, and Neesha cried out as the gun dropped to the ground before her. But she wasn't stupid. She scooped it up and aimed it across the room.

There wasn't time to check on her as he fired three more shots and dropped three more men. The last clung to his weapon and got off a rapid blast, which Jordan dodged by dropping to his knee and shooting out the other man's gun hand.

Jordan let out a low growl as he spun toward the last man standing. But he wasn't where Jordan had last seen him.

Neesha was still on the ground, her eyes wide and trembling fingers holding the gun, looking over his shoulder with an expression of shock and horror. And that's when Jordan knew. He didn't even have to turn around.

Amy was going to die.

And he was going to be sick. His stomach heaved, and he physically had to force himself to turn around.

There he was—the fifth man. The inside man. The one who had been playing them from the start. Xavier. He was decked out in a white uniform and wore a scowl on his face as he held

Amy in front of him. Her head lolled to the side, but her eyelids fluttered like she was fighting hard to recover consciousness.

His heart stopped when Xavier shifted enough to reveal the gun pointed directly at her carotid artery.

"Let her go." Jordan tried to get the words around the lump in his throat, but they came out strangled. Clearing his throat, he tried again. "What kind of man are you? You'd use a defenseless woman as a shield? Let her go."

"Somerton." Xavier cinched his arm tighter around Amy, and she groaned. "You think she's defenseless? She took out three of my guys downstairs and took off with the kid who was supposed to be my leverage. Elaina Torres was the key to getting our whole operation back up and running." He swore heavily, and spit sprayed out of his mouth with every word, as his eyes narrowed. His trigger finger bent, almost ready to pull it back and end Amy's life.

"The two of you have ruined everything! We had a plan. Get the girl off the ship, force her dad to use his connections to have Abkar extradited back to Lybania and get back in business." Xavier's eyes flashed, and his nostrils flared. "Don't you get it?"

"Get what?" Jordan asked, trying to stall. "What did we ruin?"

"Ha! Like I'm going to talk to you while you're holding a gun on me? Not likely."

Attack now or keep him calm? Jordan made a split-second decision and prayed that it was the right one.

Holding up his hands, palms facing out, he squatted and set his guns on the deck. Neesha sobbed behind him, but he never took his eyes off Xavier. "Okay. Look. I'm not armed anymore. Let her go."

"Her? *Her?* You really think I'll let her go? Don't you see? It was her stupid arrest that nearly shut us down." Spittle flew, and Amy flinched. Jordan was torn between being relieved she was waking up and terrified that she'd move at the wrong moment and cause Xavier's trigger finger to squeeze.

Oh, God, please let her be okay.

"We had a good thing going. Lybanian drugs coming in on cargo ships, transferred to my cruise ship and delivered to ports across the Caribbean. I was going to retire a wealthy man. And then she went and arrested Abkar and impounded all that cargo." His eyes bugged out. "Close to three hundred million dollars. And I was due to get ten percent. Do you know what I could have done with thirty mil?"

"Is there any on the ship now?"

"What?" Xavier's mouth dropped open,

confusion washing over his face as though he wasn't sure what or how much he'd just revealed. "That's just not… We're not talking about… That's not the thing—"

He jammed his gun into Amy's neck again, and that was it.

Jordan couldn't wait a moment longer.

But just as he launched himself at Xavier, Amy's fist came out of nowhere, her elbow a fulcrum, her knuckles nailing him in the nose.

Xavier's gun clattered to the deck as Jordan collided with them both, and they ended in a messy, bloody tangle of limbs. Xavier wailed as blood gushed down his face, which had turned a terrible shade of purple. He cursed violently, calling Amy every name in the book.

That was enough of that.

Jordan wrapped his paw around Xavier's throat and squeezed. It shut the man up, all right. He dug his fingernails into Jordan's wrist, but the pain didn't even register.

It was a gentle touch on his other arm that stopped him. "Jordan. Don't." Amy's words were barely a croak, but they were everything.

Flinging Xavier to the ground in a heap, he scooped her into his arms, holding her close and whispering into her hair, "You're okay, right? Did they hurt you?"

"My throat—" She couldn't get out more

without an audible swallow. "I'm sorry. I'm sorry I didn't meet you."

She was sorry? What a crazy world this had become that she would apologize for being kidnapped by drug runners and missing their meeting.

"I don't care if you're ten years late. Just always come back to me."

She nodded into his shoulder, resting there as the announcement he'd hoped for finally came.

"*Summer Seas*, this is the United States Coast Guard. Prepare to be boarded."

FIFTEEN

"You're such an idiot sometimes." Neesha smacked his arm, a little too hard to be playful.

Jordan rubbed at the bruise on his biceps, although he'd lost track of just when he'd sustained it on this cruise. "What's that supposed to mean?"

She rolled her eyes at him and primped her hair, pausing just briefly to admire the diamonds in the wedding band on her left hand. "Just what I said. A perfectly incredible woman is in love with you, and you're about to let her just walk away."

"I'm not *letting* her do anything. She has a mind of her own, you know?"

"Of course I know that. Which is why she's so amazing. Well, that and she has great taste in friends." She pointed at herself. "Case in point."

Jordan nodded, but couldn't manage a smile of confirmation as he stared over the ship's railing at the Miami port. They were just an hour away from exiting this cruise, which had been the opposite of the planned floating frivolity. In fact, the only thing that had gone as planned was that Neesha and Rodney had gotten hitched.

She'd been radiant as she asked the captain— after he'd been found and released from the room where Xavier had drugged and stashed him—to please do the honors. The ship had to return to Miami, and the cruise line would be paying dearly for this in lawsuits and poor press, probably for years. The least the captain could do was perform the ceremony.

Which he'd done with pride as the Coast Guard vessel escorted them home.

At least Neesha had gotten her happy ending.

But Jordan wasn't going to get his own. No matter what Neesha said.

Amy didn't want him. Now that they were safe, Elaina was with her father and Abkar's cohorts were in the custody of the Coast Guard and headed to trial, Amy didn't need him.

And even if she was remotely interested, she'd never be satisfied with what he could offer. Which was likely a broken heart.

Neesha bumped his shoulder with her own. "What's going on in your head?"

"Nothing for you to worry about."

She slammed a hand against her hip and leaned the other against the railing, turning to face his profile. "Don't treat me like I'm a child. I've been married a lot longer than you have."

He snorted. Figured. Neesha would be quick to rub it in his face that she'd gotten married before him. "Of course. How could I be so stupid?"

Her eyes turned soft as she rested a gentle hand on his arm. "Jordan, you're practically my brother, so you can't hide much from me. I saw how you looked at Amy when you held her."

"How? How did I look?" Rats. He had a sneaking suspicion that he already knew, and he wasn't really interested in confirmation.

"Like you'd do anything for her. Like you never wanted to let her go." A flicker of a smile crossed her face. "Like you're so much in love with her that you don't even know how to deal with it."

Leaning both elbows on the rail, he hunched over and scrubbed his bent head. "So what if I am? It's not going to change anything."

She flung her head back and crowed with delight. "For a really smart man, you can be really obtuse."

"Yes, we've covered that."

She got right into his face, her deep brown eyes blazing. "You're right. It won't change just *anything*. Love changes *everything*."

"It can't."

"Why not?"

He flung a hand out to the sea. "You know about my schedule. It's unpredictable and—"

"That's the most pathetic excuse, and you know it. Why on earth wouldn't you go after what you want?" Her voice rose half an octave, her glare accusing him of being a coward.

"Because it's none of your business." Sweat beaded on the back of his neck, and he took a deep breath, trying to calm down.

Haughty and so confident she knew what he was thinking, she began again, "That's ridiculous—"

"Because I could die. Because she could end up just like my mom."

Neesha slammed on the brakes, her jaw dropping open and eyes unblinking.

"What? Isn't that ridiculous enough for you?" He hated the sarcasm dripping from his voice, but it was too late to reel the words back in.

Thankfully she ignored his snide remark, planting her hand on top of his. "Do you really believe that?"

He didn't dare look at her. "My dad didn't come home from a day on the force, and my mom just…withered. She gave up on life. And I'm not going to be the reason that anyone else would do that. I won't risk breaking her heart."

"First of all—" she wagged a finger right in

his face "—if you think for one minute that you could die and no one would be hurt, you're delusional. My mother would grieve you like her own child, and you know it."

"Tha—"

"No. You're going to hear this, you big lug. And you're going to understand. People love you. Like really, really love you. Like there would be weeping and gnashing of teeth of biblical proportions if anything ever happened to you. But that's *never* going to stop us from loving you. We're not going to miss out on caring for you and spending time with you just because you happen to have a dangerous job. We're just going to pray for you and tell you to be careful and thank God every time you come home. Got it?"

His tongue was a twisted mess, and his pulse roared in his ears so loudly that he could barely nod.

"Second—and this is important, so pay attention—I know that what happened to your mom was really hard on you, and I'm sorry that losing your dad broke her. But Amy is nothing like your mom. She's the toughest woman I've ever known."

He opened his mouth to respond—although he had no words at the ready. But Neesha cut him off with a three-fingered wave.

"And third, if you think you haven't already broken Amy's heart, you're blind and stupid."

He blinked, searching for anything to say. But there was only the hammering of his heart against his rib cage and the air that he couldn't seem to find with each labored gasp.

She couldn't be right.

Not about all of it.

But he'd never known Neesha to be wrong. She was a know-it-all in the best sense of the word, aware and empathetic. And at the moment, right in his face.

The backs of his eyes burned, and he shoved the heels of his hands against them. If what she'd said was true, then he was passing on someone who filled his spirit and brought him so much joy for absolutely no reason.

None.

He was making them both miserable. For nothing.

He *was* stupid.

Amy wadded up a T-shirt and chucked it into her suitcase, ignoring the sizzle down her spine that demanded to know where all of her meticulous organizational training had gone.

Well, it might as well be on the bottom of the ocean as far as she was concerned.

No number of wrinkle-free tops or perfectly

folded maid-of-honor dresses could change the fact that she'd stood next to her best friend on Neesha's happiest day and watched the love of her own life completely ignore her.

A searing pain slashed down her chest, and she had to lean over, pressing her hands to her knees to manage even a single breath.

This. This was why she'd been so careful never to let a man deep into her heart. This ache that felt like it would last forever was reason enough to keep the wall of protection high and well preserved.

But it turned out that wanting to protect her heart and actually doing so were two different things. She could want every single brick she'd stacked in place to still be there. But Jordan had already taken them down, one by one.

And he'd been so surreptitious about it that she hadn't realized it was too late until putting the wall back together wasn't an option.

Which basically left her with perpetually leaking eyes, a running nose and a throbbing pain somewhere near where the wall had been.

Oh, and completely without Jordan because…

Well, because he didn't want her.

She crumpled another shirt and threw it into the bag as hard as she could. Stupid heartache.

"Wow, did that shirt insult your mom?"

She jerked upright and spun, a ball of shorts in her hand.

Jordan leaned in the door frame of her cabin, his shoulders stretching the cotton knit of his own shirt. He had a half smile in place, but she couldn't stand to look at it for long. It only increased the pressure in her chest.

Turning back to her packing, she said, "What are you doing here?" A thought slammed into her mind, and she swung back in his direction. "Did something happen with Xavier or Stein? Did they escape?"

His face flashed surprise, but he quickly shook his head. "No. Nothing like that. They're both still in Coast Guard custody. All of them are."

"Good." She cringed just thinking about the lot of them. Eighteen terrorists—fourteen Lybanian nationals and four Americans, including Xavier—had been part of the plot to kidnap Elaina and blackmail Michael into using his position to arrange to have Abkar extradited to Lybania. The American government didn't negotiate with terrorists, but Lybania's unstable government would happily release one back into their country.

And the terrorists had done it all so they could return to what sounded like a very lucrative drug-running business. And when Amy had rescued Elaina, they had had to come up with a plan B—threatening Neesha and Rodney in order to flush out Michael, along with Amy and Jordan.

She hadn't planned on putting a stop to a drug ring while on vacation, but maybe she could mark this as a bonus on her DEA evaluation. Perhaps at least one good thing had come of this whole ordeal.

Actually two. She'd never seen Michael so affectionate and caring toward Elaina, who was eating it up like she was starving. And maybe she had been—for love, anyway.

A warmth flowed through her chest just thinking of how much attention Elaina would enjoy from here on out. Amy prayed it would last forever.

Suddenly she remembered that Jordan was still standing there, staring at her, and shivers raced from her neck to her legs. She tried to shake them off. "Did you need something?"

"Yeah, actually, I do." He crossed his arms, and a scowl fell into place.

"What?" The word snapped out harshly—which he deserved, given his grumpy face and suddenly unpleasant attitude. "You don't have to look so sour. You're the one who came looking for me." She scooped her socks out of the dresser drawer and dumped them into the suitcase just to give herself something to do, but she couldn't turn her back on him.

He didn't bother responding to her sharp comment. "Do you actually unpack your things when you're away from home?" His eyebrows dipped low.

"Sometimes. If I think I could be called away, then I don't bother. But it wasn't like I could be called off the ship. Why? Don't you ever unpack?"

"I've lived out of a footlocker or duffel for almost half my life. Packed is my default. But I could be flexible with that."

"What?" His words didn't make any sense. Why was he telling her this? Why should she care if he unpacked or not? She was fully planning on avoiding him for the rest of her life. And all of a sudden she just needed him to go. Every minute he stood there, being all Jordan without being *her* Jordan, a sliver of her heart shriveled.

"I need to finish getting ready," she said, as dismissively as she could, glancing at him only out of the corner of her eye. "Can this wait?"

He shook his head once, definitively. "No."

Biting her tongue to keep from snapping at him again, she took a breath before asking, "What is it, then?"

"I owe you an apology."

So they'd made it back to this again? Well,

it was probably better to get it over with now. After all, she'd decided the bitterness was too heavy to carry. She'd been released from that weight, and Jordan deserved to be freed, too.

"Thank you." She looked back at her suitcase so she didn't have to watch his reaction. "I forgive you. I never should have held on to my anger from before for so long. I'm sorry for refusing your apologies. I was really angry with my dad, who used to make plans with me and then call and cancel at the last minute. When you did that, it just brought back a lot of painful memories. But I never should have taken it out on you. Let's forget that that almost date ever happened. Okay?"

He didn't say anything, and she finally peeked at him. His arms were still folded, but his head was cocked to the side, confusion written across his features.

What now? She glanced toward the ceiling and prayed for wisdom because this man was nearly enough to drive her to insanity. What more could she do?

"I...I'm glad to hear that. I guess."

He guessed? *Guessed?* He'd been badgering her for nearly a year with apologies, and now he sounded like he wasn't sure he even wanted her forgiveness.

She threw up her hands before slamming

them onto her hips and marching toward him. She stopped with just a foot between them.

"What is it that you want?"

"You."

She felt as if she'd been hit with a sledge-hammer. It had to be that because she suddenly couldn't breathe or think or process. But he kept talking like it all made perfect sense.

"You're incredible, and I was so stupid to push you away all this time." He dipped his head and swiped his big hand across the back of his neck. "I was..." He stopped, seemed to think about his words and tried again. "My dad was a cop."

"I know."

"And one day, he didn't come home." He swallowed loudly, his Adam's apple bobbing, and she couldn't not reach for his hand. But before she got there, he grabbed hers and squeezed. "My mom just broke after that. It was like the woman who I'd known and loved wasn't there anymore—like we buried all the important parts of her along with my dad. All that was left was just a shell. She couldn't care for me. She tried to, but I was mostly left on my own. And that's when Aunt Phyllis stepped in. You know the rest."

She began to nod but stopped. "What happened to your mom after that?"

His eyes glistened, and she felt like she'd waded into waters too personal, but his hold on her hand never wavered. "She died about fifteen years ago. Until then she lived in a home with others who had lost touch with reality. She never returned to her old self. All because my dad died."

Suddenly puzzle pieces began falling into place. "Jordan, you don't think…"

He nodded. "I have a dangerous job, and I can't promise that I'll always make it home. I want to. I'll try as hard as I can. But…"

"You thought that you couldn't be in a relationship because you didn't ever want to hurt someone the way your mom was hurt." She didn't even pose it as a question, and confirmation washed across his face in the form of relief.

"Stupid, right?"

"No! Who told you that?"

"Neesha."

The backs of her eyes began to burn, and she blinked furiously. "She's wrong. It's not stupid. It's kind and protective and so many other things that I love about you. But you don't have to worry about it. At least not with me."

Oh, no. That had just popped out without any planning.

He hadn't said that he loved her. But he *had* said he wanted her.

She held her breath, waiting for a response, praying he wouldn't turn and run.

He didn't. Instead he smiled.

"I know. Neesha told me that, too. And she *was* right about that."

Her heart stopped altogether, and she gasped for breath under a sudden and wonderful pressure in her chest. "Jordan?" She didn't even know what she was asking him, but he seemed to understand.

Pulling her hand to his mouth, he pressed his lips to the back of it, and lightning flashed up her arm. "Amy Delgado, I am sorry about that date that I missed, but I'm more sorry that I missed seeing you—seeing us for what we could be—for so long. You're the most incredible woman I've ever known, and you saved me more times than I can count in the last few days. I want to watch your back and have you watch mine for the rest of our lives.

"And I really, really wouldn't mind another one of those kisses."

She giggled like a teenager because what else could she do when the man she loved with all the pieces of her heart had proven that he could put it back together?

Wiggling her eyebrows at him, she said, "Did you have an ETA for that kiss?"

He stepped closer and put her hand on his

shoulder. When she walked her fingers over to his neck, she could feel his entire body tremble.

He pressed his forehead to hers and drew in a deep breath. "I think it's only fair to tell you that I'm a little bit in love with you."

She wrinkled her nose. "Only a little bit?"

He chuckled from somewhere deep in his chest. "More like a lot bit."

"I'm okay with that." She closed her eyes, only a breath between them, and everything inside her zinged in anticipation. Wrapping her hand into his shirt, she pulled him closer until they were almost sharing the same breath, but it wasn't quite enough.

"And will you be okay with it if I'm called away at a moment's notice? Like, if I'm called to a specific Middle Eastern country to meet your brother-in-law and take out the leader of a terrorist cell on a night when I'm supposed to be meeting you?"

"Are you serious?" She shoved at his chest, but his arm around her waist kept her in place. "Why didn't you just tell me?"

"I have no idea what you're talking about." But there was a twinkle in his eye that belied the truth. He'd missed their date because he had been called up on a mission. Not with the rest of his team, but as a sniper to stop a man bent on killing innocent Americans.

"No matter what," she promised him.

His hand snaked into her hair, cupping the back of her head and holding her close. "I love you, Amy." Her heart soared until she couldn't even see the remnants of the wall he'd taken down.

He leaned in to make that final connection, his lips soft and urgent and filled with promises to come. The pain, the heartache, the trials had all been worth it to be in his arms and know that she could trust him with her heart.

And she would.

"I love you, too. Always have."

One eyebrow popped up. "Always?"

She shrugged. "Longer than I'd like to admit."

He laughed and pulled her close again. "I thought you hated me."

"We have plenty of time to talk about that later."

And they did.

EPILOGUE

Seven months later

Amy snatched her purse from the passenger seat of her little coupe and tumbled out the door. The San Diego street was lined with the familiar vehicles of the SEAL Team Fifteen families, but Jordan's truck wasn't among them.

Because he'd called her to tell her he wasn't going to make it to the party this afternoon. The navy had extended his deployment another two weeks.

She'd keep waiting for him to return, but she didn't have to like it. She rolled her eyes at the memory of his phone call as she ran up the front walk to Tristan and Staci Sawyer's home. They were hosting the monthly get-together for the members of the team and their wives and children, mostly because they had a backyard big enough for all the kids to run around in.

And there were so many kids.

From Will and Jess's six-month-old all the way up to Matt and Ashley's son, Jasper, who was almost nine, the SEAL team had ended up with enough kids to form a football team. And given the size of most of their dads, these kids could take on any opponent.

She swung open the door and turned to throw her purse on the bench in the entryway, where it always went, already calling out her greeting. "Hey, guys, Jordan's not going to make it. He's not back from…"

Her voice trailed off as she slowly surveyed the empty living room. No sign of Staci or Tristan or any of the other guys and their wives. Not even a peep from the kids.

All was silent, and it made her spine tingle.

"Guys? Staci? Ashley?"

She nearly reached for her holster, but she'd left it at home. Because this was a party, and no one was after her.

She peeked up the stairs, but there was no sound there. And then she ducked into the kitchen. Trays of burgers and hot dogs and potato salad lined the counter, but no one was eating or even hovering around the food—the way the men usually did when their wives were still setting things up.

Something was really off. She'd never seen these guys pass up food.

"Hello? Is anyone here?" She poked her head into the garage, but it was empty, too, except for Tristan's truck.

Her stomach began to churn, and she wrapped her arms around her middle. All the usual sounds of laughter, chatter and children playing in the backyard were absent.

Still, she opened one of the French doors and stuck her head through.

There, on the grass in front of a semicircle of his SEAL team and their families—more quiet and still than she'd ever seen them—knelt Jordan.

"I thought you weren't..."

And then it struck her just what she was looking at. Jordan wore a tie and slacks, and there was something in his hand that sparkled as the Southern California sun caught it. "Jordan, what's..."

He didn't move much. Just a nod of his head really, but it was enough. And suddenly she ran toward him, falling to her knees before him and throwing her arms around his neck—bumping into his outstretched hand.

"I haven't even asked you yet," he teased.

"I don't care." She half laughed, half sobbed into his neck, and his arms swept around her. He'd been gone for nearly six months on deployment, and now he was back. And that was all that really mattered. Everything else was icing on the cupcake.

"Well, I do. I want to marry you, Amy Delgado. What do you think?"

"Really? You couldn't be more romantic?" She bit into her lip, trying and failing to keep her smile at bay.

He gestured to the families behind him. To the smiling fathers, beaming mothers and kids barely containing their excitement. They bounced and danced and waved at her, the little girls whispering loud enough for all to hear. "Say yes. Say yes!"

Everyone laughed, and Jordan said, "Well, I did get this all together so I could surprise you."

"I suppose, if you went to so much trouble, I can't refuse."

"I'll take it!" He slid the ring onto her finger before planting a kiss on her in front of their entire audience. And all pretense of decorum vanished. The other SEALs hooted and hollered while their wives gushed, and the kids laughed and screamed and ran off to play.

Later, while Amy stood hand in hand with her fiancé, she leaned into his shoulder, so thankful that she'd given up her grudge and learned to love.

Without Jordan, she'd have missed out on friendships with these amazing people. Ashley Waterstone, who had taken over as director of Pacific Coast House, a shelter for battered women, had become a good friend. And while her husband, Matt, had retired from the SEAL teams last month, he was busy flipping houses and caring for their three children.

Tristan Sawyer, a SEAL instructor at Coronado, and his wife, Staci, had to run to keep up with their four adopted children, but Staci always had a smile on her face as though the frantic life of a mom of four under eight was everything she'd always wanted.

Will and Jess Gumble had welcomed their first child right after the New Year, and had eagerly offered to let Amy babysit any time she liked. Will was still on active duty, but Jess didn't seem to mind. She would spend several months with her little one before returning to her work in the laboratory as a vaccination specialist.

Luke and Mandy Dunham had two of their own kids, who looked just like their dad. Luke had returned to active duty following his knee injury, and he showed no sign of retiring soon. Mandy had sold her physical therapy practice after their first baby was born and loved being a stay-at-home mom.

And Zach and Kristi McCloud were Amy and Jordan's closest friends. So far, Zach's talk of retirement because their third child was on the way hadn't gotten Jordan thinking along the same lines. But Amy wondered if it wasn't far away. It didn't matter to her. As long as he was doing work that fulfilled him, she'd be happy. She trusted the strength of their love and knew they could overcome any challenges together—especially with this support network of people to help them through it all.

It was something special, this family that Jordan had brought her into. And she'd have hated missing out on the laughter and teasing of this wild group.

But mostly she'd have hated to miss out on Jordan.

Stretching up, she kissed his cheek.

"What was that for?"

"Because I'm so glad I don't hate you anymore."

A grin spread over his face, and he leaned close. "You can't be any happier about that than I am."

* * * * *

Dear Reader,

Thank you for joining Jordan and Amy and me on this adventure. I hope you enjoyed reading their story as much as I enjoyed writing it. In fact, I've loved writing about all of the men of SEAL Team Fifteen, these men of valor.

When I wrote the first book in the series more than five years ago, I had no idea that I'd get to explore the lives of all six of these amazing men, but I've loved discovering their humor, their personalities and their matches. Love has a way of changing us, but only if we open ourselves up to it.

I hope you'll open your heart to love—especially the love of God, which is greater than we can ever imagine.

Thanks for spending your time with us. I'd love to hear from you. You can reach me at liz@lizjohnsonbooks.com, Twitter.com/LizJohnsonBooks or Facebook.com/LizJohnsonBooks. Or visit LizJohnsonBooks.com to sign up for my newsletter.

Liz Johnson

Get 2 Free Books,
Plus 2 Free Gifts—
just for trying the Reader Service!

Love Inspired®

YES! Please send me 2 FREE Love Inspired® Romance novels and my 2 FREE mystery gifts (gifts are worth about $10 retail). After receiving them, if I don't wish to receive any more books, I can return the shipping statement marked "cancel." If I don't cancel, I will receive 6 brand-new novels every month and be billed just $5.24 for the regular-print edition or $5.74 each for the larger-print edition in the U.S., or $5.74 each for the regular-print edition or $6.24 each for the larger-print edition in Canada. That's a saving of at least 13% off the cover price. It's quite a bargain! Shipping and handling is just 50¢ per book in the U.S. and 75¢ per book in Canada.* I understand that accepting the 2 free books and gifts places me under no obligation to buy anything. I can always return a shipment and cancel at any time. The free books and gifts are mine to keep no matter what I decide.

Please check one:
☐ Love Inspired Romance Regular-Print (105/305 IDN GLWW) ☐ Love Inspired Romance Larger-Print (122/322 IDN GLWW)

Name _____ (PLEASE PRINT) _____

Address _____ Apt. # _____

City _____ ·State/Province _____ Zip/Postal Code _____

Signature (if under 18, a parent or guardian must sign)

Mail to the **Reader Service:**
IN U.S.A.: P.O. Box 1341, Buffalo, NY 14240-8531
IN CANADA: P.O. Box 603, Fort Erie, Ontario L2A 5X3

Want to try two free books from another line?
Call 1-800-873-8635 today or visit www.ReaderService.com.

*Terms and prices subject to change without notice. Prices do not include applicable taxes. Sales tax applicable in N.Y. Canadian residents will be charged applicable taxes. Offer not valid in Quebec. This offer is limited to one order per household. Books received may not be as shown. Not valid for current subscribers to Love Inspired Romance books. All orders subject to approval. Credit or debit balances in a customer's account(s) may be offset by any other outstanding balance owed by or to the customer. Please allow 4 to 6 weeks for delivery. Offer available while quantities last.

Your Privacy—The Reader Service is committed to protecting your privacy. Our Privacy Policy is available online at www.ReaderService.com or upon request from the Reader Service.

We make a portion of our mailing list available to reputable third parties that offer products we believe may interest you. If you prefer that we not exchange your name with third parties, or if you wish to clarify or modify your communication preferences, please visit us at www.ReaderService.com/consumerchoice or write to us at Reader Service Preference Service, P.O. Box 9062, Buffalo, NY 14240-9062. Include your complete name and address.

LI17R2